ALSO BY ELMORE LEONARD

ELMORE LEONARD

The Hot Kid

HarperLargePrint

An Imprint of HarperCollins*Publishers*

THE HOT KID. Copyright © 2005 by Elmore Leonard, Inc. All rights reserved. Printed in the United States of America. No part of this book may be used or reproduced in any manner whatsoever without written permission except in the case of brief quotations embodied in critical articles and reviews. For information address HarperCollins Publishers Inc., 10 East 53rd Street, New York, NY 10022.

HarperCollins books may be purchased for educational, business, or sales promotional use. For information please write: Special Markets Department, HarperCollins Publishers Inc., 10 East 53rd Street, New York, NY 10022.

FIRST HARPER LARGE PRINT EDITION

Printed on acid-free paper

Library of Congress Cataloging-in-Publication Data
Leonard, Elmore, 1925–
   The hot kid: a novel / Elmore Leonard.— 1st ed.
     p.   cm.
   ISBN 0-06-072422-6 (Hardcover)
   1. Police—Oklahoma—Fiction. 2. Oklahoma—Fiction. I. Title.

PS3562.E55H66 2005
13'.54—dc28   2004063578

ISBN 0-06-078716-3 (Large Print)

05 06 07 08 09 WBC/RRD 10 9 8 7 6 5 4 3 2 1

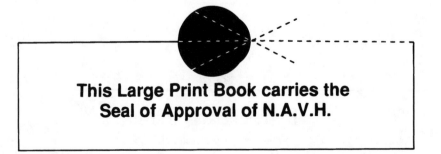

**This Large Print Book carries the
Seal of Approval of N.A.V.H.**

For my two girls,
Jane and Katy

1

Carlos Webster was fifteen the day he witnessed the robbery and killing at Deering's drugstore. This was in the fall of 1921 in Okmulgee, Oklahoma.

He told Bud Maddox, the Okmulgee chief of police, he had driven a load of cows up to the yard at Tulsa and by the time he got back it was dark. He said he left the truck and stock trailer across the street from Deering's and went inside to get an ice cream cone. When he identified one of the robbers as Emmett Long, Bud Maddox said, "Son, Emmett Long robs banks, he don't bother with drugstores no more."

Carlos had been raised on hard work and respect for his elders. He said, "I could be wrong," knowing he wasn't.

They brought him over to police headquarters in the courthouse to look at photos. He pointed to Emmett Long staring at him from a $500 wanted bulletin and picked the other one, Jim Ray Monks, from mug shots. Bud Maddox said, "You're positive, huh?" and asked Carlos which one was it shot the Indian. Meaning Junior Harjo with the tribal police, who'd walked in not knowing the store was being robbed.

"Was Emmett Long shot him," Carlos said, "with a forty-five Colt."

"You sure it was a Colt?"

"Navy issue, like my dad's."

"I'm teasing," Bud Maddox said. He and Carlos' dad, Virgil Webster, were buddies, both having fought in the Spanish-American War and for a number of years were the local heroes. But now doughboys were back from France telling about the Great War over there.

"If you like to know what I think happened," Carlos said, "Emmett Long only came in for a pack of smokes."

Bud Maddox stopped him. "Tell it from the time you got there."

Okay, well, the reason was to get an ice cream cone. "Mr. Deering was in back doing prescriptions—he looked out of that little window and told me to help myself. So I went over to the soda fountain and scooped up a double dip of peach on a sugar cone and went to the cigar counter and left a nickel by the cash register. That's where I was when I see these two men come in wearing suits and hats I thought at first were salesmen. Mr. Deering calls to me to wait on them as I know the store pretty well. Emmett Long comes up to the counter—"

"You knew right away who he was?"

"Once he was close, yes sir, from pictures of him in the paper. He said to give him a deck of Luckies. I did and he picks up the nickel I'd left by the register. Hands it to me and says, 'This ought to cover it.'"

"You tell him it was yours?"

"No sir."

"Or a pack of Luckies cost fifteen cents?"

"I didn't say a word to him. But see, I think that's when he got the idea of robbing the store, the cash register sitting there, nobody around but me holding my ice cream cone. Mr. Deering never came out from the back. The other one, Jim Ray Monks, wanted a tube of Unguentine, he said for a heat rash was bothering him, under his arms. I got it for him and he didn't pay either. Then Emmett Long says, 'Let's see what you have in the register.' I told him I didn't know how to open it as I didn't work there. He leans over the counter and points to a key—the man knows his cash registers—and says, 'That one right there. Hit it and she'll open for you.' I press the key—Mr. Deering must've heard it ring open, he calls from the back of the store, 'Carlos, you able to help them out?' Emmett Long raised his voice saying, 'Carlos is doing fine,' using my name. He told me then to take out the scrip but leave the change."

"How much did he get?"

"No more'n thirty dollars," Carlos said. He took his time thinking about what happened right after, starting with Emmett Long looking at his ice cream cone. Carlos saw it as personal, something between him and the famous bank robber, so he skipped over it, telling Bud Maddox:

"I put the money on the counter for him, mostly singles. I look up—"

"Junior Harjo walks in," Bud Maddox said, "a robbery in progress."

"Yes sir, but Junior doesn't know it. Emmett Long's at the counter with his back to him. Jim Ray Monks is over at the soda fountain getting into the ice cream. Neither of them had their guns out, so I doubt Junior saw it as a robbery. But Mr. Deering sees Junior and calls out he's got his mother's medicine. Then says for all of us to hear, 'She tells me they got you raiding Indian stills, looking for moonshine.' He said something about Junior setting a jar aside for him and that's all I heard. Now the guns are coming out, Emmett Long's Colt from inside his suit . . . I guess all he had to see was Junior's badge and his sidearm, that was enough, Emmett Long shot him. He'd know with that Colt one round would do the job, but he stepped up and shot Junior again, lying on the floor."

There was a silence.

"I'm trying to recall," Bud Maddox said, "how many Emmett Long's killed. I believe six, half of 'em police officers."

"Seven," Carlos said, "you count the bank hostage had to stand on his running board. Fell off and broke her neck?"

"I just read the report on that one," Bud Maddox said. "Was a Dodge Touring, same as Black Jack Pershing's staff car over in France."

"They drove away from the drugstore in a Packard," Carlos said, and gave Bud Maddox the number on the license plate.

Here was the part Carlos saw as personal and had skipped over, beginning with Emmett Long looking at his ice cream cone.

Then asking, "What is that, peach?" Carlos said it was and Emmett Long reached out his hand saying, "Lemme have a bite there," and took the cone to hold it away from him as it was starting to drip. He bent over to lick it a couple of times before putting his mouth around a big bite he took from the top dip. He said, "Mmmmm, that's good," with a trace of peach ice cream along the edge of his mustache. Emmett Long stared at Carlos then like he was studying his features and began licking the

⌐one again. He said, "Carlos, huh?" cocking his head to one side. "You got the dark hair, but you don't look like any Carlos I ever seen. What's your other name?"

"Carlos Huntington Webster, that's all of 'em."

"It's a lot of name for a boy," Emmett Long said. "So you're part greaser on your mama's side, huh? What's she, Mex?"

Carlos hesitated before saying, "Cuban. I was named for her dad."

"Cuban's the same as Mex," Emmett Long said. "You got greaser blood in you, boy, even if it don't show much. You come off lucky there." He licked the cone again, holding it with the tips of his fingers, the little finger sticking out in a dainty kind of way.

Carlos, fifteen years old but as tall as this man with the ice cream on his mustache, wanted to call him a dirty name and hit him in the face as hard as he could, then go over the counter and bulldog him to the floor the way he'd put a bull calf down to brand and cut off its balls. Fifteen years old but he wasn't stupid. He held on while his heart beat against his chest. He felt the need to stand up to this man, saying finally, "My dad was a marine on the battleship **Maine** when she was blown up in Havana Harbor, February fifteenth, 1898. He survived, was picked up in the water and thrown in a Spanish prison as a spy. Then when he escaped he fought the dons on the side of the insurrectionists, the rebels. He fought them again and was wounded at Guantánamo, with Huntington's Marines in that war in Cuba where he met my mother, Graciaplena Santos."

"Sounds like you daddy was a hero," Emmett Long said.

"I'm not done," Carlos said. "After the war my dad came back home and brought my mother with him when Oklahoma was still Indian Territory. She died having me, so I never knew her. I never met my dad's mother, either. She's Northern Cheyenne, lives on a reservation out at Lame Deer, Montana," saying it in a voice that was slow and calm compared to what he felt inside. Saying, "What I want to ask you—if having Indian blood, too, makes me something else besides a greaser." Saying it in Emmett Long's face, causing this man with ice cream on his mustache to squint at him.

"For one thing," Emmett Long said, "the Indin blood makes you and your daddy breeds, him more'n you." He kept staring at Carlos as he raised the cone, his little finger sticking out, Carlos thinking to lick it again, but what he did was toss the cone over his shoulder, not looking or caring where it would land.

It hit the floor in front of Junior Harjo just then walking in, badge on his tan shirt, revolver on his hip, and Carlos saw the situation turning around. He felt the excitement of these moments but with some relief, too. It picked him up and gave him the nerve to say to Emmett Long, "Now you're gonna have to clean up your mess." Except Junior wasn't pulling his .38, he was looking at the ice cream on the linoleum and Mr. Deering was calling to him about his mother's medicine and about raiding stills and Emmett Long was turning from the counter with the Colt in his hand, firing, shooting Junior Harjo and stepping closer to shoot him again.

There was no sign of Mr. Deering. Jim Ray Monks came over to have a look at Junior. Emmett Long laid his Colt on the glass counter, picked up the cash in both hands and shoved the bills into his coat pockets before looking at Carlos again.

"You said something to me. Geronimo come in and you said something sounded smart aleck."

Carlos said, "What'd you kill him for?" still looking at Junior on the floor.

"I want to know what you said to me."

The outlaw waited.

Carlos looked up rubbing the back of his hand across his mouth. "I said now you'll have to clean up your mess. The ice cream on the floor."

"That's all?"

"It's what I said."

Emmett Long kept looking at him. "You had a

gun you'd of shot me, huh? Calling you a greaser. Hell, it's a law of nature, you got any of that blood in you you're a greaser. I can't help it, it's how it is. Being a breed on top of it—I don't know if that's called anything or not. But you could pass if you want, you look enough white. Hell, call yourself Carl, I won't tell on you."

Carlos and his dad lived in a big new house Virgil said was a California bungalow, off the road and into the pecan trees, a house that was all porch across the front and windows in the steep slant of the roof, a house built a few years before with oil money—those wells pumping away on a half-section of the property. The rest of it was graze and over a thousand acres of pecan trees, Virgil's pride, land gathered over the years since coming home from Cuba. He could let the trees go and live high off his oil checks, never work again as long as he lived. Nothing doing—harvesttime Virgil was out with his crew gathering pecans, swiping at the branches with cane fishing poles. He had Carlos tending the cows, fifty, sixty head of cross-Brahmas at a time grazing till they filled out good and Carlos would drive a bunch at a time to market in the stock trailer.

He told his dad every time he went to Tulsa some

wildcatter would offer to buy his truck and trailer, or want to hire him to haul pipe out to the field. Carlos said, "You know I could make more money in the oil business than feeding cows?"

Virgil said, "Go out to a rig and come back covered in that black muck? That sound good to you? Son, we can't spend the money we have."

Oklahoma became a state in 1907—Carlos was one year old—and they started calling Tulsa "The Oil Capital of the World." A man from Texas Oil came down from the Glenn Pool fields near Tulsa and asked Virgil if he wanted to be rich. "You notice that rainbow in your creek water? You know that's a sign of oil on your property?"

Virgil said, "I know when the Deep Fork overflows it irrigates my pe-can groves and keeps out the weevils."

Still, he wouldn't mind some extra money and leased Texas Oil the half section they wanted for a one-eighth share and a hundred dollars a year per working well. The discovery hole hit a gusher a quarter mile into the earth, and Virgil found himself making nine to twelve hundred dollars a day for most of the next few years. Texas Oil offered to lease his entire spread, 1,800 acres, and Virgil turned them down. Seeing gushers spewing crude over his pecan trees didn't give him the thrill it did Texas Oil.

When Carlos got back from a haul Virgil would be sitting on that big porch with a bottle of Mexican beer. Prohibition was no bother, Virgil had a steady supply of the Mexican beer and American bourbon brought here by the oil people. Part of the deal.

The night Carlos witnessed the robbery and killing he sat with his old dad and told him the whole story, including what he'd left out of his account to Bud Maddox, even telling about the ice cream on Emmett Long's mustache. Carlos was anxious to know if his dad thought he might've caused Junior Harjo to get shot. "I don't see how," Virgil said, "from what you told me. I don't know why you'd even think of it, other than you were right there and what you're wondering is if you could've prevented him from getting shot."

Virgil Webster was forty-seven years old, a widower since Graciaplena died in ought-six giving him Carlos and requiring Virgil to look for a woman to nurse the child. He found Narcissa Raincrow, sixteen, a pretty little Creek girl related to Johnson Raincrow, deceased, an outlaw so threatening that peace officers shot him while he was sleeping. Narcissa had lost her own child giving birth, wasn't married, and Virgil hired her on as a wet nurse. By the time little Carlos had lost interest in her breasts, Virgil had acquired an appreciation. Narcissa became their housekeeper now and began sleeping in Virgil's bed. She cooked good, put on some weight but was still pretty, listened to Virgil's stories and loved and appreciated him. Carlos loved her, had fun talking to her about Indian ways and her murderous kin, Johnson Raincrow, but never called her anything but Narcissa. Carlos liked the idea of being part Cuban; he saw himself wearing a panama hat when he was older, get one side of it to curve up a little.

He said to his dad that night on the dark porch, "Are you thinking I should've done something?"

"Like what?"

"Yell at Junior it's a robbery? No, I had to say something smart to Emmett Long. I was mad and wanted to get back at him somehow."

"For taking your ice cream cone?"

"For what he said."

"What part was it provoked you?"

"What **part**? What he said about being a greaser."

"You or your mama?"

"Both. And calling me and you breeds."

Virgil said, "You let that bozo irk you? Probably

can't read nor write, the reason he has to rob banks. Jesus Christ, get some sense." He swigged his Mexican beer and said, "I know what you mean though, how you felt."

"What would you have done?"

"Same as you, nothing," Virgil said. "But if you're talking about in my time, when I was still a U.S. Marine? I'd of shoved the ice cream cone up his goddamn nose."

Three days later sheriff's deputies spotted the Packard in the backyard of a farmhouse near Checotah, the house belonging to a woman by the name of Crystal Lee Davidson. Her former husband, Byron "Skeet" Davidson, deceased, shot dead in a gun battle with U.S. marshals, had at one time been a member of the Emmett Long gang. The deputies waited for marshals to arrive, as apprehending armed fugitives was their specialty. The marshals slipped onto the property at first light, fed the dog a wiener, tiptoed into Crystal's bedroom and got the drop on Emmett Long before he could dig his Colt from under the pillow. Jim Ray Monks went out a window, started across the barn lot and caught a load of double-ought in his legs that put him down. The two were brought to Okmulgee and locked up to await trial.

Carlos said to his dad, "Boy, those marshals know their stuff, don't they? Armed killer—they shove a gun in his ear and yank him out of bed."

He was certain he'd be called to testify and was anxious, couldn't wait. He told his dad he intended to look directly at Emmett Long as he described the cold-blooded killing. Virgil advised him not to say any more than he had to. Carlos said he wondered if he should mention the ice cream on Emmett Long's mustache.

"Why would you want to?" Virgil said.

"Show I didn't miss anything."

"You know how many times the other night," Virgil said, "you told me about the ice cream on his mustache? I'm thinking three or four times."

"You had to see it," Carlos said. "Here's this bank robber everybody's scared of, doesn't know enough to wipe his mouth."

"I'd forget that part," Virgil said. "He shot a lawman in cold blood. That's all you need to remember about him."

A month passed and then another, Carlos becoming fidgety. Virgil found out why it was taking so long, came home to Narcissa putting supper on the table, Carlos sitting there, and told them the delay was caused by other counties wanting to get their hands on Emmett Long. So the matter was given to the Eastern District Court judge to rule on, each county laying out its case, sounding like they'd make a show out of trying him. "His Honor got our prosecutor to offer Emmett Long a deal. Plead guilty to murder in the second degree, the motive self-defense as the victim was armed, and give him ten to fifty years. That would be the end of it, no trial needed. In other words," Virgil said, "your Emmett Long will get sent to McAlester and be out in six years or so."

"There was nothing self-defense about it," Carlos said. "Junior wasn't even looking at him when he got shot." Carlos sounding like he was in pain.

"You don't know the system," Virgil said. "The deal worked 'cause Junior's Creek. He was a white man Emmett Long'd get life or a seat in the electric chair."

Another event of note took place when Carlos was fifteen, toward the end of October and late in the afternoon, dusk settling in the orchards. He shot and killed a cattle thief by the name of Wally Tarwater.

Virgil's first thought: it was on account of Emmett Long. The boy was ready this time and from now on would always be ready.

He phoned the undertaker, who came with sheriff's people and pretty soon two deputy U.S.

marshals arrived, Virgil knowing them as serious lawmen in their dark suits and the way they wore their felt hats down on their eyes. The marshals took over, the one who turned out to be the talker saying this Wally Tarwater—now lying in the hearse—was wanted on federal warrants for running off livestock and crossing state lines to sell to meat packers. He said to Carlos to go on and tell in his own words what happened.

Virgil saw Carlos start to grin just a little, about to make some remark like "You want it in my own words?" and cut him off quick with "Don't tell no more'n you have to. These people want to get home to their families."

Well, it began with Narcissa saying she felt like a rabbit stew, or squirrel if that's all was out there. "I thought it was too late in the day," Carlos said, "but took a twenty-gauge and went out in the orchard. The pecans had been harvested, most of 'em, so you could see through the trees good."

"Get to it," Virgil said. "You see this fella out in the pasture driving off your cows."

"On a cutting horse," Carlos said. "You could tell this cowboy knew how to work beef. I got closer and watched him, admiring the way he bunched the animals without wearing himself out. I went back to the house and exchanged the twenty-gauge for a Winchester, then went to the barn and saddled up.

She's right over there, the claybank. The sorrel's the one he was riding."

The marshal, the one who talked, said, "You went back to get a rifle without knowing who he was?"

"I knew it wasn't a friend stealing my cows. He's driving them down toward the Deep Fork bottom where a road comes in there. I nudge Suzie out among the cows still grazing, got close enough to call to him, 'Can I help you?'" Carlos started to smile. "He says, 'Thanks for offering but I'm done here.' I told him he sure was and to get down from his horse. He started to ride away and I fired one past his head to bring him around. I moved closer but kept my distance not knowing what he had under his slicker. By now he sees I'm young, he says, 'I'm picking up cows I bought off your daddy.' I tell him I'm the cow outfit here, my dad grows pecans. All he says is, 'Jesus, quit chasing me, boy, and go on home.' Now he opens his slicker to let me see the six-shooter on his leg. And now way off past him a good two hundred yards, I notice the stock trailer, a man standing there by the load ramp."

"You can make him out," the marshal who did the talking said, "from that distance?"

"If he says it," Virgil told the marshal, "then he did."

Carlos waited for the marshals to look at him

before saying, "The cowboy starts to ride off and I call to him to wait a second. He reins and looks at me. I told him I'd quit chasing him if he brought my cows back. I said, 'But you try to ride off with my stock I'll shoot you.'"

"You spoke to him like that?" the talker said. "How old are you?"

"Going on sixteen. The same age as my dad when he joined the U.S. Marines."

The quiet marshal spoke for the first time. He said, "So this Wally Tarwater rode off on you."

"Yes sir. Once I see he isn't gonna turn my cows, and he's approaching the stock trailer by now, I shot him." Carlos dropped his tone saying, "I meant to wing him, put one in the edge of that yellow slicker . . . I should've stepped down 'stead of firing from the saddle. I sure didn't mean to hit him square. I see the other fella jump in the truck, doesn't care his partner's on the ground. He goes to drive off and tears the ramp from the trailer. It was empty, no cows aboard. What I did was fire at the hood of the truck to stop it and the fella jumped out and ran for the trees."

The talkative marshal spoke up. "You're doing all this shooting from what, two hundred yards?" He glanced toward the Winchester leaning against a pecan tree. "No scope on your rifle?"

"You seem to have trouble with the range," Virgil said to him. "Step out there a good piece and hold up a snake by its tail, a live one. My boy'll shoot its head off for you."

"I believe it," the quiet marshal said.

He brought a card from his vest pocket and handed it between the tips of his fingers to Virgil. He said, "Mr. Webster, I'd be interested to know what your boy sees himself doing in five or six years."

Virgil looked at the card and then handed it to Carlos, meeting his eyes for a second. "You want you can ask him," Virgil said, watching Carlos reading the card that bore the deputy's name, R. A. "Bob" McMahon, and a marshal's star in gold you could feel. "I tell him join the marines and see foreign lands, or get to love pe-cans if you want to stay home." He could see Carlos moving his thumb over the embossed star on the card. "The only thing he's mentioned is maybe getting a job in the oil fields once he finishes high school," Virgil said, looking at his boy.

"Isn't that right?"

Virgil and the marshals waited the few moments before Carlos raised his head to look at his dad.

"I'm sorry—were you speaking to me?"

Later on Virgil was in the living room reading the paper. He heard Carlos come down from upstairs and said, "Will Rogers is appearing at the Hippodrome next week. He talks about current events while he's showing off with his rope. You care to see him? He's funny."

"I guess," Carlos said, then told his dad he didn't feel so good.

Virgil lowered the newspaper to look at his boy. He said, "You took a man's life today." And thought of a time in Cuba behind an overturned oxcart looking down the barrel of a Krag rifle pressed to his cheek, wanting the first one coming toward him riding hard—his friend being chased by the three behind him—to get out of the way, get the hell out of his line of fire, and he did, swerved his mount, and Virgil put his sights on the first one coming behind him and fired, felt the Krag kick against his shoulder and saw the horse tumble headfirst on top of the rider, threw the bolt and put his sights on the second one, **bam,** took the rider out of his saddle, threw the bolt and aimed at the third one coming like a racehorse, the rider firing a revolver as fast as he could thumb the hammer, a brave man set on riding him down, twenty yards between them when Virgil blew him out of his saddle and the horse ran past the overturned oxcart. He'd killed three men in less than ten seconds.

He said to Carlos, "You didn't tell me, did you look at him lying there?"

"I got down to close his eyes."

Virgil had taken the boots off the third one he killed, exchanged them for the sandals he'd worn in the Spanish prison, the Morro.

He said, "Looking at him made you think, huh?"

"It did. I wondered why he didn't believe I'd shoot."

"He saw you as a kid on a horse."

"He knew stealing cows could get him shot or sent to prison, but it's what he chose to do."

"You didn't feel any sympathy for the man?"

"Yeah, I felt if he'd listened he wouldn't be lying there dead."

The room was silent. Now Virgil asked, "How come you didn't shoot the other one?"

"There weren't any cows on the trailer," Carlos said, "else I might've."

It was his son's quiet tone that made Virgil realize, My Lord, but this boy's got a hard bark on him.

2

Jack Belmont was eighteen years old in 1925, the time he got the idea of blackmailing his dad.

This was the year the Mayo Hotel opened in Tulsa, six hundred rooms with bath, circulating ice water that came out of the faucet. They knew Jack at the Mayo and never said anything about his stopping by to get a bottle of booze off the bellboy. It cost him more this way, but was easier than dealing with bootleggers. Drive up in his Ford Coupé and honk the horn, tell the doorman to go get Cyrus. That was the old colored bellboy's name. Sometimes Jack went inside to hang around the lobby or the Terrace Room, see what was going on. It was how he found out this was where his dad, Oris Belmont, kept his girlfriend when she came to visit, at the Mayo. The girlfriend being what the blackmail was about.

Her name was Nancy Polis from Sapulpa, a boomtown in the Glenn Pool grid, barely ten miles from Tulsa.

Jack believed his dad must visit her when he went

out to the oil field and stayed the night. He figured his dad was worth ten million or so by now, except it wasn't all sitting in the bank; it was invested in different things like a refinery, a car lot, a tank farm, and a trucking line. It was boom or bust in the oil business, the reason Oris Belmont spread his money around, and why Jack wasn't sure how much to ask for blackmailing him.

He chose a number that sounded good and entered the dad's private study at home, fixed the way Oris wanted it: steer horns over the fireplace, photos of men posing by oil derricks, also miniature rigs, little metal derricks on the mantel, on bookshelves, one used as a doorstop. Jack walked up to the big teakwood desk and sat down in soft leather across from Oris, the dad.

"I don't want to take up your time," Jack said. "What I'd like you to do is put me on your payroll. I'm thinking ten thousand a month and I won't bother you no more."

Eighteen years old and talking like that.

Oris set his desk pen in its holder and gave this good-looking, useless boy who favored his mother his full attention.

"You aren't saying you're going to work, are you?"

"I'll come by once a month," Jack said, "on payday."

Oris said, "Oh, I see," easing back in his chair,

"this is a shakedown. All right, I pay you more'n the president of the Exchange National Bank makes . . . or what?"

"I know about your girlfriend," Jack said.

The dad said, "Is that right?"

"Nancy Polis. I know all about your putting her up at the Mayo when she comes to visit. I know you always come in through that outside entrance to the barbershop in the basement and have a drink before you go up to her room, always the same one. I know you and your oil friends have blocks of ice in the urinals, and you bet on who can make the deepest hole pissing on 'em, and you never win."

"Who told you all this?"

"One of the bellboys."

"The one gets whiskey for you?"

Jack hesitated. "A different one. I told him to keep an eye out and call me when she comes in the hotel. I've seen her in the lobby and recognized her right away."

"What's all this information cost you?"

"Couple of bucks. Dollar for her name and address, how she registers. A girl in the office told the bellboy you pay the bill whenever she stays, usually every other Friday through the weekend. I know you met her when you were living in Sapulpa those years we never saw you."

The dad said, "You're sure of that, huh?"

"I know you bought her a house, set her up."

The dad's droopy mustache gave him a tired look staring across the desk, the way Jack saw the dad whenever he thought of him. The big mustache, the suit and tie, and that tired look, rich as he was.

"Let's see," the dad said, "you were five when I came out here to work."

"You left us I was four years old."

"Well, I know you were ten when I bought this house. Fifteen in 1921, the time you took my pistol and shot that colored boy."

Jack looked at him surprised. "Everybody was shooting niggers, the race riot was going on. I didn't kill him, did I?"

"That whole neighborhood of Greenwood burned down—"

"Niggerville," Jack said. "Was the Knights of Liberty started the fires. I know I told you back then I never struck a match."

"What I'm trying to recall," the dad said, "the first time you were arrested."

"For shooting out streetlights."

"And assault. You got picked up for getting that little girl drunk and raping her. Carmel Rossi?"

Jack started shaking his head saying she wasn't any little girl. "You'd seen the titties on her you'd of known she was grown up. She dropped the charge, didn't she?"

"I paid her daddy what he makes in a month."

"She had her panties hanging over a bush before I ever touched her. Was my word against hers."

"Her daddy still works for me," Oris said. "Builds storage tanks, the big ones, hold fifty-five and eighty thousand barrels of crude. How'd you like to work for him, clean out tanks? Get in there in the fumes and shovel out that bottom sludge. Start there and we work you up to your ten thousand a month."

"Everything I got into," Jack said, sitting low in the leather chair, comfortable, "either I didn't start it or it was a misunderstanding."

"How about getting caught with the Mexican reefer? What didn't the police understand about it?"

Jack grinned at the dad.

"You ever try it?"

See what the dad had to say to that.

Nothing. He said, "I don't know what's wrong with you. You're a nice-looking boy, wear a clean shirt every day, keep your hair combed . . . Where'd you get your ugly disposition? Your mama blames me for not being around, so then I feel guilty and give you things, a car, whatever you want. You get in trouble, I get you out. Well, now you've moved on to extortion in your life of crime. What're we talking about here? I pay what you want or you're telling everybody I have a girlfriend?

Jesus Christ, you know how many girlfriends there are in Tulsa? Set up with their own place? Hell, I keep mine in Sapulpa. Is that the deal, you're threatening to tell on me?"

"I tell Mama," Jack said, "see how you like her knowing."

Now he was getting the cold stare again, Jack ready to pick up the metal derrick from the corner of the desk if Oris came at him. Be self-defense.

But the dad didn't move. He said, "You think your mama doesn't know about her?"

Shit. Jack hadn't thought of that.

Still, Oris could be bluffing.

"All right," Jack said, "I'll tell her I know about it, too. And I'll see if I can get Emma to understand you're screwing this oil camp whore."

He thought it would set Oris off, get him yelling—the idea of his little Emma hearing such a thing, even though she had no sense of things. The dad stayed calm across the desk and it surprised Jack, the bugger staring, but holding on like that.

When Oris did speak the dad's voice seemed different, delivering a judgment now with no more to say about it.

"You tell your mother she'll hate you for knowing it and never be able to look at your face again. She'll tell me you have to leave and I won't hesitate. I'll throw you out of the house." He didn't refer to

Emma. But then gave him a choice, still his dad saying, "Is that what you want?"

Oris Belmont was another wildcatter story.

Glenn Pool had twelve hundred wells piped and flowing to refineries by the time Oris came to Oklahoma to join his wife's Uncle Alex in Sapulpa. Alex Roney, known in the field as Stub, held mineral leases on Creek Indian land, a scattering of half-sections he'd bought for three dollars an acre before the area came into its boom. By the time it did, Stub was broke, had no means of drilling a discovery well. He was drunk the day he highjacked a tank truck of crude, was caught stuck hub-deep in mud and spent the next four years doing his time at McAlester. Stub got his release and called Oris Belmont. Oris arrived from Indiana with a load of salvaged drilling tools, pipe, casing, a pair of steam boilers, sixteen hundred dollars he'd scraped together and twenty years of oil stain under his fingernails.

They drilled two dry holes, Stub No. 1 and No. 2, and the old uncle's luck ran out on him. They were looking to take the No. 2 derrick apart, Stub up on the runaround, the catwalk that circled the derrick sixty or so feet up. He hadn't yet hooked his safety belt to the structure, and when he lost his hold he fell sixty feet to the drilling floor, his final breath smelling of corn whiskey. Oris had been afraid the old uncle might fall or have something fall on his head.

What puzzled Oris were the dry holes. There weren't more than twenty in the entire eight thousand acres of wells and two of them were his. What Oris did, he got mad, changed the name of the company from Busy Bee Oil & Gas—a cartoon bumblebee in the trademark they'd of had one day—to NMD Oil & Gas, standing for No More Dusters, and worked a year as a driller to restore his capital. Now he sank Emma No. 1, named for his baby girl he'd seen twice in the past four years, and sweet crude came up and came up like there'd never be an end to it.

Oris's wife was from Eaton, Indiana, where they'd met while he was working for wages in the Trenton Field. Oris and Doris—he told her they were meant to be joined in marriage. The time came to hook up with her uncle in Oklahoma, Doris was ready to have their third child—three counting Oris Jr., who'd died in infancy of diphtheria. So Doris and their little boy Jack stayed in Eaton with her widowed mother and delivered Emma while Oris was drilling the dusters.

When Emma No. 1 came in, bless her heart, Oris left the boardinghouse where he'd been staying and moved to the St. James Hotel in Sapulpa. He waited until he'd drilled Emma No. 2 and she was flowing before he phoned Doris.

Oris said, "Honey? Guess what?"

Doris said, "If your holes are still dry I'm leaving you. I'm walking out of here and Mama can have the kids. She's raising 'em anyway, spoiling 'em rotten. Says Emma's gonna be a nervous stability 'cause I don't know how to nurse her, I'm not patient enough. How can I be, her hanging over my shoulder. She talks to Emma, tells her, 'Suck on the titty, Little Bitty,' what she calls her. 'That's it, suck on it hard, get all that mookey.'"

Oris said, "Honey? Listen to me a minute, will you? We're becoming rich as I speak."

Doris wasn't finished but paused to hear that much. She was a farm girl, skin and bones all her life, but was strong from working; she had a cute face, good teeth, read magazines and was always respectful of her husband. Saturdays she used to shave him and trim his hair and his big droopy mustache. Then she'd strop the razor and shave her legs and under her arms, the driller twisting his mouth to one side and then the other watching every stroke and getting a boner. Doris was thirty-four by now, the driller ten years older. Saturday was their time to get cleaned up before doing the dirty. She still had a wrathful mood on her and told him, "You know you haven't seen Jack in going on five years?"

"I spent Christmases with you."

"Twice in that time, two days each. He's a harum-scarum, hell in short pants," Doris said. "I'm through trying to manage him. Emma—you haven't hardly ever seen except in pictures, and Mama's driving me crazy. You don't send me train fare right now I'm leaving you. You can come and get your kids you don't even know."

There, she'd told him.

Doris said now, "For true? We're rich?"

"Nine hundred barrels a day out of two wells," Oris said, "and we're about to drill other leases. We had to shoot Emma Number Two with nitro to bust up the rock and she came in angry, almost tore the goddamn rig down. I hired a man's building storage tanks for me." He said to Doris, "You all right? You feel better now?"

She did, but there was some wrath left and Doris said, "Jack needs his daddy to make him behave. He won't do a thing I tell him."

"Honey," Oris said, "you're gonna have to hang on there a while longer. I bought us a house on Tulsa's south side, where all the Princes of Petroleum live. Be just another month or so, I'm having the place fixed up."

She asked him what was wrong with it.

"The oilman owned it went bust. His wife left him, his second one, and he shot himself in the head, in their bedroom. I'm having it repainted. The house—they had wild parties and broke things." He said, "Honey, the house was put up for auction, the man owing taxes on it. I bought it off the county for twenty-five thousand dollars, cash."

She had never seen a house that cost twenty-five thousand dollars and asked him what it looked like. He said, "It's Greek Revival, eight years old."

She said, "I don't know Greek Revival from a teepee."

He told her it had those Doric columns in front holding up the portico, and she still didn't know what it looked like.

He told her there was a dining room could seat twenty people easy. She imagined harvest hands sitting there having noon dinner. He told her it had five bedrooms and four baths, a sleeping porch, a maid's room, three-car garage, a big kitchen that had an icebox with seven doors in it, a swimming pool in the backyard . . . "I almost forgot," Oris said, "and a roller-skating rink on the third floor."

There was a silence on the phone.

Oris said, "Honey . . . ?"

Doris said, "You know I never roller-skated in my life?"

By the summer of 1916 the Belmonts were in their Tulsa mansion, Oris trying to decide what to do about his girlfriend Nancy Polis, a waitress at the Harvey House restaurant in Sapulpa. He felt they should stop seeing each other now that he was living in Tulsa; but each time he brought it up Nancy would cry and carry on, not acting at all like what she was, a Harvey Girl. It hurt him so much he bought her the home she opened as a boardinghouse for income.

On a Sunday morning in September Oris sat with his wife on the patio having breakfast while the children played in the swimming pool. Doris was reading the Society section of the paper looking for names she recognized. Oris watched Jack, ten years old, talking to his little sis, Emma, four years younger. He watched Emma jump in the deep end of the swimming pool and now Jack jumped in and Emma was hanging on to him screaming, her tiny voice shrill but nothing new, Emma was always screaming at Jack, telling him to stop it and then yelling for her mama. Doris looked up and said, as she always did, "What's he doing to her now, the poor child." Oris said it looked like they were playing. Doris said, "She wearing her water wings?" Oris said he couldn't tell but imagined so, Emma never going in the water without her life preserver.

Doris went back to reading about neighbors and Oris picked up the Sports section. He saw the St. Louis Cardinals were still in last place in the National League, the Brooklyn Robins, goddamn it, in first, two and a half games ahead of Philly. Oris looked toward the pool again. Jack was sitting in a canvas chair wearing a pair of smoked glasses too big for his young face. Emma was nowhere in sight. Oris called out, "Jack, where's your sister?" Doris put down her paper.

Oris would see the next part clearly anytime he thought about it: Jack on his feet now looking at the pool, then seeing her under water and diving in to save her life.

She wasn't breathing when they pulled her out. Oris didn't know what to do. Doris did, she went crazy screaming and crying, asking God why He took their little girl. Sunday their doctor, who lived nearby in Maple Ridge, was home. He came right away and said, "How long has it been?" And, "Why aren't you giving her artificial respiration?"

Oris remembered Jack talking to her, Emma nodding and then jumping in the pool, not wearing her water wings, and screaming trying to hold on to Jack. Oris believed his little girl was unconscious for almost fifteen minutes before the doctor forced her to breathe again and they took her, stretched out on the backseat of the La Salle, to the hospital.

The lack of oxygen to her brain for that long meant it no longer worked the way it should. She couldn't walk. She sat in her wheelchair and stared, or crawled around the roller-skating rink upstairs scrubbing the floor with her dolls, or throwing them or beating the floor with her babies until they came apart and there were pieces of dolls all over the roller rink the Belmonts never used.

Jack talked his mother out of having the swimming pool broken up and planted over. He would catch his dad staring at him and the ten-year-old would say, "I tried to save her, didn't I?"

Eight years later the smart-aleck, useless kid was trying to blackmail him. It was time to hand Jack over to Joe Rossi at the tank farm, the daddy of Carmel, the girl Jack swore up and down he hadn't raped.

Joe Rossi had dug coal in the mines near Krebs, south of here. He served a few years at McAlester as a prison guard before the Glenn Pool boom came on and moved his family to Tulsa to find work in oil that paid a living wage. Mr. Belmont first had him digging earthen pits, big holes in the ground, someplace quick to store crude gushing out of the wells. Next thing he was setting wood tanks over the field before going to steel plates, setting tanks as high as three-story buildings, some holding eighty thousand barrels of crude before pumping it off to a refinery. Joe Rossi was making a hundred dollars a week now running the tank farm and bossing the hard cases working for him. Tankies all drank their wages, saw themselves as the toughest boys on the lease and looked for excuses to start fights. Joe Rossi had fists the size of mallets and used them on payday to stay in charge, hammer anybody told him to go fuck himself, or some such thing. He didn't mind their getting drunk, but would not take their lip.

Mr. Belmont said put the boy on the worst job there. Rossi said that was tank cleaning. He said, "You think it's what you want him to do? The only thing liable to kill a man quicker is shooting nitro."

"I want him cleaning tanks," Mr. Belmont said, and hung up the phone.

Rossi told Norm Dilworth, a boy he'd brought here from McAlester after he'd done his time, told him to show Jack Belmont the work and stay close to him. Joe Rossi didn't trust himself to go near Mr. Belmont's son—not after what he did to his little girl Carmel, the youngest of his seven kids, fifteen years old this past July 16, the feast day of Our Lady of Mount Carmel. Rossi was afraid if the boy got smart with him he'd crack his head open with a maul and shove him in the muck.

Rossi said to Norm Dilworth, not much older

than Jack Belmont, "He's the boss's son. His daddy wants him to learn the oil business."

Norm said, "Cleaning out tanks? Christ Almighty, he could die in there."

"I don't think his daddy'd mind," Rossi said. "He's a bad kid. You knew plenty like him at McAlester, only they weren't the sons of millionaires."

The two boys were lanky and looked like they could run. Jack and Norm stood smoking cigarets waiting for the setter crew to unbolt a steel plate from the bottom part of the tank that rose a good thirty feet above them, pried it free and used a truck with a chain to drag the plate out of the way. Now a thick black muck was oozing out of the opening to spread in the weeds. They could smell gas fumes coming from inside the tank.

Norm Dilworth said, "Put out your cigaret," stubbing his on the sole of a shoe and slipping the butt in his shirt pocket. Jack took another puff before he flicked his cigaret away. Jack was wearing a new pair of Pioneer bib overalls bought yesterday, complaining to the dad at the store with him they were too full in the legs. The dad bought him four pair, a buck ten each, and a pair of work shoes for three eighty-five. Norm Dilworth had on work clothes that would never look clean again but were worn out from washing, suspenders holding up his pants. He wore a hat so old and dirty you couldn't tell the shade of felt, set on the back of his head. Jack wouldn't wear a hat less he had on a suit. His brown hair was combed back and plastered down, taking on a shine in the sunlight.

"That bottom sediment's what we clean out," Norm said. "Wade inside with shovels and rakes made of wood—no metal that could cause a spark—and slosh it out the opening. You last all day you can make seven-fifty. Only if they's gas fumes like in this'n? You can't stay in there more'n ten minutes at a time. You have to come out to breathe. They's some companies tell you, 'Well, you only worked half your time,' and take out for it. You say, 'Yeah, well, the other time I was using to breathe.' It don't matter, they take breathing time out of your wage. Except Mr. Rossi, he pays a straight six bits an hour. You have to come out, he lets you come out. See, you don't want to get weak in there from the fumes. I mean it, you fall in the sludge, you're done. You keep slipping and sliding, you're choking on the gas and can't help but fall in the muck. It's like knee-deep in there, the sediment, and nobody's suppose to help you, try and pull you out, 'cause you could pull them in and you're both gone."

Jack stared at the black ooze edging toward them while Norm was staring at Jack. Norm said, "I never seen bibs that narrow in the legs. Where you buy a pair like that?"

Jack was watching the sediment coming closer and closer. "I thought the pants were too roomy. I had one of the maids take 'em in." He said, "So this Joe Rossi is fair, huh? I haven't seen him."

"He's over in the shack," Norm said. "He wrote to me at McAlester saying he'd have a job waiting for me when I got my release. So I come here and the next thing I know I got married."

Jack was looking at him now, this hick in his worn-out work clothes. "You were in prison, huh?"

"Year and a day for stealing cars, the first time."

"Now you clean tanks for six bits an hour? But you don't have to?"

"Shit, I can make forty dollars a week."

"What'd you do with the cars you swiped?"

"Sold 'em. I kept a Dodge to run bootleg till I almost got caught."

Jack was getting a better feeling about this hick who knew how to steal cars and run whiskey. "You ever think about getting back into crime?"

"I kinda miss running wild and free," Norm said, "but I've known Mr. Rossi from when he was a screw over at the prison. He's always been fair with me. Another thing about working for him, he won't use 'lectric lights when you're in the tank. The vents on the roof don't give enough light, he'll put batt'rey-powered spots up there. See, 'lectric lights, you got to worry about a current leak. Over at Seminole one time, they go in, switch on the light and she sparked. Seven men in there, the whole tank went up afire and you heard the seven of 'em scream like one person, this awful, bloodcurdling scream and like that"—Norm snapped his fingers—"they're dead. They's any kind of spark in there you're fried. Pull you out looking like a strip of bacon."

Jack said, "We the only ones working here?"

"A crew'll be coming," Norm said, and looked over at the shack where Rossi had his office, no one there yet.

Jack moved along the edge of the sediment to the opening and ducked his head to look in at a dim cavern, spooky in there, poles holding up the roof, the floor thick with sediment. He began to cough and walked back clearing his throat and blinking his eyes from the fumes.

Norm said, "See what I mean?"

"I'm not going in there," Jack said. "I got an idea I like better than getting burned alive. I'm thinking of how me and you can make a hundred thousand dollars and not even get our shoes dirty." He had the hick squinting at him now with sort of a grin on his face. "You're the guy I been looking for," Jack said, "somebody's not afraid to break a law now and then."

Norm quit grinning. "What kind of crime you have in mind?"

"Kidnap my old man's girlfriend. Tell him a hundred thousand or he'll never see her again."

Norm said, "Jesus Christ, you mean it, don't you?"

Jack nodded toward his Ford Coupé parked off the dirt road by some trucks loaded with used sheets of metal. He said, "Go on get in my car over there. You won't ever have to clean another tank long as you live."

Norm Dilworth looked toward the car and Jack pulled a pack of cigarets and his silver lighter from the overalls that felt stiff on him. Norm looked back to see him lighting the cigaret and yelled out, "No!" and said Jesus Christ, no a few more times, looking toward Rossi's office, looking at Jack puffing on the butt before he flicked it to arch into the stream of sludge.

Fire flashed and spread over the ooze out on the ground—they were both running now—the fire wooshing into the tank to ignite the gas and there was a boom inside, an explosion that buckled steel plates, blew the roof off the tank and rolled black oil smoke into the sky.

Oris Belmont saw it from his office window high up in the Exchange National Bank Building, his NMD

Oil & Gas Company occupying the whole floor. The explosion from eight miles away turned Oris in his swivel chair to see that ugly black stain in the sky, rising where his tank farm would be. He thought of his son walking out of the house this morning in his new overalls; Oris remembering the legs looked funny. In nine years there had never been an accident at the farm, not even by the hand of God like a tank struck by lightning, not until the day Jack showed up for work. Oris wasn't sure what to feel about the situation. He waited for the phone to ring.

Rossi came on to ask him, "Can you see it?"

"A full tank," Oris said, "there'd be way more smoke."

"It's one your boy was to work in."

Oris waited.

"He set fire to the sediment," Rossi said, "and drove off in his car with another tankie, I guess through for the day. If it's okay with you, I'd as soon you didn't send him back here."

Oris felt relief. He did, his boy off to work for the first time in his life was alive. It calmed him till he began to wonder, But now what?

Jack had no trouble getting Nancy Polis out of her boardinghouse and in the car, the woman not even bothering to put on a hat but did grab her

13

A few days after Jack Belmont and Heidi rented a furnished bungalow on Edgevale—**Modern, 6 rooms with sleeping porch**—an Italian-looking guy in his fifties wearing glasses, a fitted Chesterfield coat and snappy gray fedora, rang the bell and identified himself saying, "Good afternoon, I'm Teddy Ritz, welcome to Kansas City. Where might you folks be from?"

Heidi thought it was funny a guy his age calling himself Teddy and chewing gum. She said, "We might be from the North Pole, Teddy. What business is it of yours?"

Jack had noticed the second dude standing by the La Salle—a young guy, Teddy's driver or bodyguard—and could see that Teddy was somebody who didn't care for smart talk from a girl. Teddy Ritz stopped chewing his gum and stared at Heidi through his rimless glasses. He said, "Sweetheart, I'm vice president of the Democratic Club and head of all the precinct captains in Jackson County. In other words, my position is right under called since Choc got away. Am leaving this morning. I will stop at a gas station and get a map.

Love & kisses,
Louly

P.S. I am thinking of changing my name to Kitty and starting a new life.

quoted the secretary of the Oklahoma Bankers Association saying, "Floyd must be killed before he is captured."

Louly Brown, who had gone as far as the sixth grade, said, "Why capture him if he's already dead?" It surprised her that she noticed this, written by the secretary of the Bankers Association, instead of feeling heartbroken about Choc. Maybe because she was tired of thinking of him as a good guy once you got to know him. Tired of sticking up for him. She listened to **Amos 'n' Andy** and went to bed and lay there in the dark thinking of what she'd say in the note, if she felt the same in the morning.

She did. She wrote the note on Mayo Hotel stationery she'd brought with her and left it on the kitchen table with the newspaper. The note said:

Dear Carl,
I have given up on the two men I thought I admired most in the world—you and Charley Floyd. I can't wait any longer to go dancing with you and see the sights as you are always busy. The same is true of Charley Floyd. (Boy is he busy!) I have stopped letting people believe I am his girlfriend. There is no way to keep up with you two boys. I am going to Kansas City since you have not even

"You've been lucky," Carl said.

"Where's East Young?"

"I'll tell you tomorrow."

"You're gonna get him tonight?"

"Dawn, the dawn patrol swoops in."

"You're not taking part?"

"I get to watch."

"So you won't have a chance to shoot him?"

Carl paused. "Why'd you say that?"

Louly said, "I don't know," in her own head. "What about Ruby and the boy?"

"They'll be allowed to walk out."

"I can't even drive past the house?"

"They won't let you on the street. You'll have to wait and read about it in the paper."

The headline on the front page of the **World** read: OFFICERS FOILED BY "PRETTY BOY" IN GAS-BOMB RAID.

The story said that when the police tossed the tear gas bomb through the front window, Floyd and Birdwell went out the back and drove away.

There was more to the story, how the police moved into the dark house and rooted around once they found it empty. There was an editorial saying the police had blundered. Another one

The second time he came home she said, "All I do is talk to you through the bathroom door. What're you doing's so special?"

Carl said he couldn't tell her.

"Well, all I been doing every night is listening to **Amos 'n' Andy,** George Burns and Gracie Allen, Ed Wynn, or Walter Winchell talking to Mr. and Mrs. America and all the ships at sea, and you don't tell me nothing."

She gave him that the second time he was home and Carl said, "Okay, we're closing in on your boyfriend, Charley Floyd."

The words stunned Louly.

"He's here?"

"Living on East Young Street with Ruby and the boy, according to the police informant, one of the neighbors. And a guy with them the police think is George Birdwell, Choc's partner."

"All the time since they left Fort Smith," Louly said, "he's been in **Tulsa?**"

"The past month. The informant says Ruby shops at the grocery store on credit, tells them she'll settle when her husband gets paid at work. Meaning, when he robs a bank."

Louly said, "What is **wrong** with me? This is the third time I'm only a few miles from Charley Floyd and I don't know it."

"Jack hasn't been here?"

Doris said, "You know what I have under this cushion? A thirty-two caliber pistol." She wiggled her fanny to show Carl where it was. "He comes up those stairs and walks in here to kiss me on the cheek? I'm gonna shoot him and watch him bleed on the carpet."

"You tell Mr. Belmont that?"

"I told him he tries to stop me I'll shoot him, too."

In five days Louly had seen Carl Webster twice, both times when he came home to freshen up and change his clothes. They hadn't even spent the night together yet.

"Oh, you're gonna take me dancing? See the sights of Tulsa?" Using her best sarcastic tone of voice. "You know who's appearing at Cain's Ballroom all this week? The Light Crust Doughboys featuring Bob Wills. The ad in the paper calls them the hottest hillbilly swing band you'd ever want to hear. Every night the ballroom's crowded with two-steppers."

Carl told her from the bathroom, "Honey, I'm on the hottest investigation of my career, working surveillance, watching for a certain fugitive."

"You told me you were taking time off."

"I been called in special on this one."

purse. She had seen the smoke and believed Jack telling her Mr. Belmont had been hurt in the explosion and sent him to get her. Mr. Belmont wanting her to see he was alive before going to the hospital in Tulsa, as his wife was likely to show up there. No, he wasn't hurt too bad, just some cuts that'd have to be sewed up, maybe a broken leg set, if it was broke. Jack told her he worked for Mr. Belmont in the office; he'd put on overalls today as they were going out to the lease, explaining this to Nancy Polis squeezed between him and Norm Dilworth in the car on the way to Norm's house.

It was toward Kiefer in a stand of pines back of the rail yard. Nancy didn't ask why Oris would be waiting in this workingman's house of upright weathered boards, a porch roof in front, a privy in back where a girl was hanging wash. Jack asked Norm who she was. Norm said his wife, and Jack said to bring her in the house.

She was watching them now, fingering her blonde hair the wind was blowing in her eyes.

As soon as they were inside Nancy said, "Where's Oris?"

Jack told her he'd be along. Mr. Belmont had waited for the doctor they called to have a look at the tankies that got hurt. He had a feeling Nancy was suspicious now, nervous, looking around the house. There wasn't much to it, a pump on the sink, an old icebox and stove, a table covered with oilcloth and magazines sitting on it, three straight chairs, a double bed they could see in the back room.

Jack was ten when they moved to Tulsa and his dad would take him out to the lease every once in a while and explain boring things about oil wells, how the first joint of pipe had a bit on it they called a fishtail that bored the hole and those big pumps they called mud hogs would clean it out. They always stopped by the Harvey House in Sapulpa for chicken à la king, Jack's favorite, and always had the same Harvey Girl in her big white apron, her hair swept up and fixed. Jack would listen to them talk in a low voice like they were passing secret messages to each other. It wasn't until he saw Nancy Polis at the Mayo Hotel he realized she was the Harvey House waitress. She'd be in her thirties now.

Norm came in, the girl behind him with her empty clothes basket. He said to Jack, "This here's my wife, Heidi."

It took Jack by surprise, 'cause up close this girl was a looker, even with her hair mussed, no makeup on, man, a natural beauty about twenty years old. He had to wonder why she'd settled for a hayseed like Norm Dilworth. There was a presence about her, reminding him of rich girls in Tulsa, till she said, "Y'all want some ice tea?" and she was off a farm or an oil patch. Man, but she was a looker.

Nancy Polis, sitting at the table now smoking a cigaret, said, "I want to know where Oris is."

Jack was still looking at Heidi. "You got anything else?"

"I got a jar," Norm said.

Jack turned to the table and the magazines sitting there, **Good Housekeeping, Turkey World, Ladies' Home Journal** and a new issue of **Outdoor Life.** He said to Nancy, "Keep your pants on," picked up the **Outdoor Life** and started looking through it.

Norm went to the cupboard over the sink and brought out a mason jar, a third of clean whiskey in it. He said to Heidi, "Honey, will you get the glasses?"

She said, "We only got two," looking at Jack. "Somebody'll have to tip the jar."

Jack smiled at her staring at him. He held up the **Outdoor Life** and said to Norm, "You hunt?"

"Any chance I get."

"Leave this little girl here by herself?"

He winked at her and she winked back.

"She likes it here," Norm said, "after where she's lived."

Nancy said, "None for me, thanks," watching Norm pour the liquor into a couple of jelly glasses.

"It ain't for you, it's for me and Jack," Norm said, handing Jack a glass.

Nancy sat sideways to the table, her legs crossed, showing her knees and some thigh in a dark shade of hose. She looked at Jack and held out the cigaret to tap ashes on the linoleum floor.

"Are you old enough?"

"If Prohibition means nobody's suppose to drink," Jack said, "then anybody can break the law and drink if they want, can't they?"

"You work for Oris Belmont directly?"

"I'm his first assistant."

"What kind of a man is he to work for?"

Jack raised the glass Norm handed him and took a big swallow of the liquor, feeling a nice burn, Nancy staring at him. Jack said, "I won't say anything nasty about Mr. Belmont. I've heard some things but I don't know if they're true or not."

"Like what?"

"He's hard on certain employees in the office, cute girls they say he's especially hard . . . on." He winked at Nancy. Shit, he couldn't help it. He heard Norm laugh and looked over at Heidi grinning at him. He could see her nipples poking against the thin cotton dress. She knew it, too, grinning at him like a cat if a cat had tits. He turned to Nancy drawing on her cigaret, her eyes holding on him, but no smile from this one. He took another sip of the whiskey, smooth going down. He was starting to feel good already. She wasn't going anywhere—he may as well tell her.

"Honey, you're gonna be staying here a while."

She held the cigaret with his elbow on the table.

"Nothing happened to Oris?"

"I told you he was hurt to get you out of the house."

"What're you, holding me for ransom?"

"We'll see how much Mr. Belmont likes you."

"He doesn't pay, then what, you kill me?"

"He'll pay."

"Then you **will** have to kill me."

"What for? We're gone. Nobody knows where we're at."

"But I know who you are."

It stopped him and he said, "I don't work for Oris Belmont. I only told you that."

"I know you don't," Nancy said, "you're his rotten kid. As soon as this goober called you Jack I knew it. You're Jack Belmont. I remember you from eight or nine years ago when I worked at the Harvey House. You'd want to go home and you'd whine and keep tugging at your daddy's sleeve. You were a brat then, now you're what, a kidnapper? I heard the blackmail didn't work."

Shit. He did think of shooting her. It passed through his mind knowing Norm'd have a gun if he hunted.

Nancy said, "You give me the creeps, you know it? You can ask your dad for money anytime you want and he'll give it to you. No, you'd rather steal it from him. Lord have mercy, you want to be a real crook, go rob a bank."

Later on that day Joe Rossi phoned his boss again. He said, "Mr. Belmont, you want to get your boy to straighten himself out? What I'd do is have him arrested for destroying company property."

Oris Belmont didn't say a word. He sat looking out the window at the smudge still in the sky.

"You want," Joe Rossi said, "I'd be glad to call the police on him. Keep you out of it."

Oris took a few moments before saying, "No, I'll call them." It was time he took charge.

3

June 13, 1927, Carlos Huntington Webster, now close to six feet tall, was in Oklahoma City wearing a dark blue suit of clothes, no vest and a panama with the brim curved on his eyes just right, staying at a hotel, riding streetcars every day, and being sworn in as a deputy United States marshal. This was while Charles Lindbergh was being honored in New York City, tons of ticker tape dumped on the Lone Eagle for flying across the Atlantic Ocean by himself.

And Emmett Long, released from McAlester, was back in Checotah with Crystal Davidson, his suit hanging in the closet these six years since the marshals hauled him off in his drawers. The first thing the outlaw did, once he got off Crystal, was make phone calls to get his gang back together.

Carlos was given a leave to go home after his training and spent it with his old dad, telling him things:

What the room was like at the Huckins Hotel.

What he had to eat at the Plaza Grill.

How he saw a band called Walter Page's Blue
Devils that was all colored guys.

How when firing a pistol you put your weight
forward, one foot ahead of the other, so if you get
hit you can keep firing as you fall.

And one other thing.

Everybody called him Carl instead of Carlos. At
first he wouldn't answer to it and got in arguments,
a couple of times almost fistfights.

"You remember Bob McMahon?"

"R. A. 'Bob' McMahon," Virgil said, "the
quiet one."

"My boss when I report to Tulsa. He says, 'I
know you're named for your granddaddy to honor
him, but you're using it like a chip on your shoulder instead of a name.'"

Virgil was nodding his head. "Ever since that
moron Emmett Long called you a greaser. I know
what Bob means. Like, 'I'm Carlos Webster,
what're you gonna do about it?' You were little I'd
call you Carl sometimes. You liked it okay."

"Bob McMahon says, 'What's wrong with Carl?
All it is, it's a nickname for Carlos.'"

"There you are," Virgil said. "Try it on."

"I've been wearing it the past month or so. 'Hi,
I'm Deputy U.S. Marshal Carl Webster.'"

"You feel any different?"

"I do, but I can't explain it."

A call from McMahon cut short Carl's leave. The Emmett Long gang was back robbing banks.

What the marshals tried to do over the next six months was anticipate the gang's moves. They robbed banks in Shawnee, Seminole and Bowlegs on a line south. Maybe Ada would be next. No, it turned out to be Coalgate.

An eyewitness said he was in the barbershop as Emmett Long was getting a shave—except the witness didn't know who it was till later, after the bank was robbed. "Him and the barber are talking, this one who's Emmett Long mentions he's planning on getting married pretty soon. The barber happens to be a minister of the Church of Christ and offers to perform the ceremony. Emmett Long says he might take him up on it and gives the reverend a five-dollar bill for the shave. Then him and his boys robbed the bank."

Coalgate was on that line south, but then they turned around and headed north again. They took six thousand from the First National in Okmulgee but lost a man. Jim Ray Monks, slow coming out of the bank on his bum legs, was shot down in the street. Before Monks knew he was dying he told them, "Emmett's sore you never put more'n five hundred on his head. He's out to show he's worth a whole lot more."

The stop after Okmulgee was Sapulpa, the gang appearing to like banks in oil towns: hit three or four in a row and disappear for a time. There were reports of gang members spotted during these periods of lying low, but Emmett Long was never one of them.

"I bet anything," Carl said, standing before the wall map in Bob McMahon's office, "he hides out in Checotah, at Crystal Davidson's house."

"Where we caught him seven years ago," McMahon said, nodding. "Crystal was just a girl then, wasn't she?"

"I heard Emmett was already fooling with her," Carl said, "while she's married to Skeet, only Skeet didn't have the nerve to call him on it."

"You heard, huh."

"Sir, I drove down to McAlester on my day off, see what I could find out about Emmett."

"The convicts talk to you?"

"One did, a Creek use to be in his gang, doing thirty years for killing his wife and the guy she was seeing. The Creek said it wasn't a marshal shot Skeet Davidson in the gun battle that time, it was Emmett himself. He wanted Skeeter out of the way so he could have Crystal for his own."

"What made you think of her?"

"Was after that barber in Coalgate said Emmett

spoke about getting married. I thought it must be Crystal he's talking about. I mean if he's so sweet on her he killed her husband? That's what tells me he hides out there."

Bob McMahon said, "Well, we been talking to people, watching every place he's ever been seen. Look it up, I know Crystal Davidson's on the list."

"I did," Carl said. "She's been questioned and Checotah police are keeping an eye on her place. But I doubt they do more than drive past, see if Emmett's drawers are hanging on the line."

"You're a marshal six months," Bob McMahon said, "and you know everything."

Carl didn't speak, his boss staring at him.

McMahon saying after a few moments, "I recall the time you shot that cattle thief off his horse." McMahon saying after another silence but still holding Carl with his stare, "You have some kind of scheme you want to try?"

"I've poked around and learned a few things about Crystal Davidson," Carl said, "where she used to live and all. I believe I can get her to talk to me."

Bob McMahon said, "How'd you become so sure of yourself?"

The Marshals Service occupied offices on the second floor of the United States Courthouse on

South Boulder Avenue in Tulsa. This meeting in Bob McMahon's office was the first time Jack Belmont's name came up in conversation: Bob McMahon and Carl Webster deciding it was between the bank robberies in Coalgate and Sapulpa that Jack must've got out of prison and joined the Emmett Long gang.

What was different about the Sapulpa bank robbery, Emmett Long walked in and first tried to cash a check made out to him for ten thousand dollars, a NMD Gas & Oil check bearing the signature of Oris Belmont, the company president. Jack Belmont, standing at the teller's window with Emmett, said, "That's my daddy signed it. I give you my word the check's good." The teller reported that he recognized Jack Belmont from his dad bringing him in since he was a kid, but the signature didn't look anything like Oris Belmont's on file. It didn't matter, by then Emmett and Jack Belmont had their revolvers out, as did another one of the gang later identified as Norm Dilworth, and the tellers cleaned out what was in their drawers, something over twelve thousand dollars.

Bob McMahon asked Carl if he knew about Jack Belmont, how he'd set fire to one of his dad's storage tanks, Jack and this tankie named Dilworth, a former convict. The dad didn't hesitate to point Jack out in court. Joe Rossi identified Norm, and the two boys were convicted of malicious destruction of property, each drawing two years hard time.

Carl said he'd read it in the paper and spoke to the Tulsa police about Jack's previous arrests. "And I saw him at McAlester," Carl said, "to find out what I could learn about Emmett Long."

He told how they sat in the captain's office off the rotunda that must be four stories high, where the east and west cell houses met. "You hear wings beating," Carl said, "and look up to see a pigeon flying around inside."

He told how Jack sat across the desk from him in a lazy kind of way like he wasn't interested, his legs crossed like a girl's. "He smoked the cigaret I gave him and stared at me, wouldn't say he even knew Emmett, but this had to be where they first met. Emmett was already out when Jack got his release, right after I spoke to him. So they must've already decided to hook up and do some banks. I can hear Jack telling Emmett he had a new way to rob them, hand 'em a check to cash."

McMahon said, "And I bet Emmett kicked his tail."

"But tried the check first," Carl said. "I'm talking to him, Jack sat there with one arm folded across his chest to the other arm tight against his body, holding the cigaret straight up between the tips of his fingers. He'd turn his head to take a drag, his face raised to it like he's showing me his profile."

"You mentioned his legs crossed like a girl's," McMahon said. "You think he's a nancy-boy?"

"At first I did. I said, 'There fellas here gonna have fun with you.' But he did have girlfriends and was accused of raping one, though he was never brought up. He said he didn't give the other inmates a second thought. He had his buddy with him, Norm Dilworth doing his second stretch and Norm, Jack said, had showed him how to jail. I'm told this Dilworth is stringy but tough as nails. No," Carl said, "Jack Belmont was putting on a show, letting me know he was cool as a fifty-pound block of ice. He asked me what I was, even though I'd showed him my star. I said I was a deputy United States marshal. He called me a poor sap and wanted to know if I'd ever shot anybody."

"You tell him?"

"I said just one. He shrugged like it wasn't anything special. I told him the next time I saw Emmett Long he'd be my second one."

Bob McMahon didn't care for that. He said, "I reminded you once before, my deputies don't brag or speculate. The hell got into you to say that?"

"The way he looked at me," Carl said. "The way

he smoked the cigaret. Different things about his manner toward me."

Carl watched Bob McMahon shake his head, McMahon saying, "My deputies do not brag on themselves. Have you got that?"

Carl said he did.

But thinking that Jack Belmont, with what he was up to now, could be number three.

Marshals dropped Carl off a quarter mile from the house, turned the car around and drove back to Checotah; they'd be at the Shady Grove Café. Carl was wearing work clothes and curl-toed boots, his .38 Colt Special holstered beneath a limp old suitcoat of Virgil's, a black one, his star in a pocket.

Walking the quarter mile his gaze held on this worn-out homestead, the whole dismal 160 acres looking deserted, the dusty Ford Coupé in the backyard abandoned, its wheels missing. Carl expected Crystal Davidson to be in no better shape than her property, living here like an outcast. The house did take on life as he mounted the porch, the voice of Uncle Dave Macon coming from a radio somewhere inside; and now Crystal Lee Davidson was facing him through the screen, a girl in a silky nightgown that barely came to her knees, barefoot, but with rouge giving her face color, her blonde hair marcelled like a movie star's . . .

You dumbbell, of **course** she hadn't let herself go, she was waiting for a man to come marry her. Carl smiled, meaning it.

"Miz Davidson? I'm Carl Webster." He kept looking at her face so she wouldn't think he was trying to see through her nightgown, which he could, easy. "I believe your mom's name is Atha Trudell? She worked at the Georgian Hotel in Henryetta doing rooms at one time and belonged to Eastern Star?"

It nudged her enough to say, "Yeah . . . ?"

"So'd my mom, Narcissa Webster?"

Crystal shook her head.

"Your daddy was a coal miner up at Spelter, pit boss on the Little Gem. He lost his life that time she blew in '16. My dad was down in the hole laying track." Carl paused. "I was ten years old."

Crystal said, "I just turned fifteen," her hand on the screen door to open it, but then hesitated. "Why you looking for me?"

"Lemme tell you what happened," Carl said. "I'm at the Shady Grove having a cup of coffee? The lady next to me at the counter says she works at a café serves way better coffee'n here. Purity, up at Henryetta."

Crystal said, "What's her name?"

"She never told me."

"I use to work at Purity."

"I know, but wait," Carl said. "The way you came up in the conversation, the lady says her husband's a miner up at Spelter. I tell her my dad was killed there in '16. She says a girl at Purity lost her daddy in that same accident. She mentions knowing the girl's mom from Eastern Star, I tell her mine belonged, too. The waitress behind the counter's pretending not to listen, but now she turns to us and says, 'The girl you're talking about lives right up the road there.'"

"I bet I know which one it was," Crystal said. "She have spit curls like that boop-oop-a-doop girl?"

"I believe so."

"What else she say?"

"You're a widow, lost your husband."

"She tell you marshals gunned him down?"

"Nothing about that."

"It's what everybody thinks. She mention any other names?"

What everybody thinks. Carl put that away and said, "No, she got busy serving customers."

"You live in Checotah?"

He told her Henryetta, he was visiting his old grandma about to pass. She asked him, "What's your name again?" He told her and she said,

"Well, come on in, Carl, and have a glass of ice tea." Sounding now like she wouldn't mind company.

There wasn't much to the living room besides a rag rug on the floor and stiff black furniture, chairs and a sofa, their cane seats giving way from years of being sat on. The radio was playing in the kitchen. Crystal went out there and pretty soon Carl could hear her chipping ice. He stepped over to a table laid out with magazines, **True Confession, Photoplay, Liberty, Western Story,** and one called **Spicy.**

Her voice reached him asking, "You like Gid Tanner?"

Carl recognized the radio music. He said, "Yeah, I do," as he looked at pictures in **Spicy** of girls doing housework in their underwear, one girl wearing a teddy up on a ladder with a feather duster.

"Gid Tanner and his Skillet Lickers," Crystal's voice said. "You know who I kinda like? That Al Jolsen, he sure sounds like a nigger on that mammy song. But you want to know who my very favorite is?"

Carl said, "Jimmie Rodgers?" looking at pictures of Joan Crawford and Elissa Landi now in **Photoplay.**

"I like Jimmy o-**kay** . . . How many sugars?"

"Three'll do'er. How about Uncle Dave Macon? He was on just a minute ago."

"'Take Me Back to My Old Carolina Home.' I don't care for the way he half-sings and half-talks a song. If you're a singer you oughta sing. No, my favorite's Maybelle Carter and the Carter Family. The pure loneliness they get in their voices just tears me up."

"Must be how you feel," Carl said, "living out here."

She came out to hand him his cold drink saying, "Don't give it another thought."

"Sit here by yourself reading magazines . . ."

"Honey," Crystal said, "you're not as cute as you think you are. Drink your ice tea and beat it."

"I'm sympathizing with you," Carl said. "The only reason I came, I wondered if you and I might even've known each other from funerals, and our moms being in the same club. That's all." He smiled just a little saying, "I wanted to see what you look like."

Crystal said, "All right, you **are** cute, but don't get nosy."

She left him with his iced tea and went in the bedroom.

Carl took **Photoplay** across the room to sit in a chair facing the table of magazines and the bedroom door, left open. He turned pages in the magazine. It wasn't a minute later she stuck her head out.

"You've been to Purity, haven't you?"

"Lot of times."

She stepped into plain sight now wearing a sheer, peach-colored teddy, the crotch sagging between her white thighs. Crystal said, "You hear about the time Pretty Boy Floyd came in?"

"While you were working there?"

"Since then, not too long ago. The word got around Pretty Boy Floyd was at Purity and it practically shut down the whole town. Nobody'd come out of their house." She stood with hands on her hips in kind of a slouch. "I did meet him one time. Was at a speak in Oklahoma City."

"You talk to him?"

"Yeah, we talked about . . . you know, different things." She looked like she might be trying to think of what they did talk about, but said then, "Who's the most famous person you ever met?"

He wasn't expecting the question. Still, he thought about it for no more than a few seconds before telling her, "I guess it would have to be Emmett Long."

Crystal said, "Oh . . . ?" like the name didn't mean much to her. Carl could tell, though, she was being careful, on her guard.

"Was in a drugstore when I was a kid," Carl said, "and he came in for a pack of Luckies. I'd stopped there for a peach ice cream cone, my favorite. You know what Emmett Long did? Asked could he have a bite—this famous bank robber."

"You give him one?"

"I did, and you know what? He kept it, wouldn't give me back my cone."

"He ate it?"

"Licked it a few times and threw it away." Carl didn't mention the trace of ice cream on the bank robber's mustache; he kept that for himself. "Yeah, he took my ice cream cone, robbed the store and shot a policeman. You believe it?"

She seemed to nod, thoughtful now, and Carl decided it was time to come out in the open.

"You said people think it was marshals gunned down your husband, Skeet. But you know better, don't you?"

He had her full attention, staring at him now like she was hypnotized.

"And I'll bet it was Emmett himself told you. Who else'd have the nerve? I'll bet he said you ever leave him he'll hunt you down and kill you. On account of he's so crazy about you. I can't think of another reason you'd stay here these years. You have anything to say to that?"

Crystal began to show herself, saying, "You're not from a newspaper . . ."

"Is that what you thought?"

"They come around. Once they're in the house they can't wait to leave. No, you're not at all like them."

Carl said, "Honey, I'm a deputy United States marshal. I'm here to put Emmett Long under arrest or in the ground, one."

He worried she might've acquired an affection for the man, but it wasn't so. Once Carl showed her his star Crystal sat down and breathed with relief. Pretty soon her nerves did take hold and she became talkative. Emmett had phoned this morning and was coming. Now what was she supposed to do? Carl asked what time she expected him. She said going on dark. A car would drive past and honk twice; if the front door was open when it drove past again Emmett would jump out and the car would keep going.

Carl said he'd be sitting here reading about Joan Crawford. He said to introduce him as a friend of the family happened to stop by, but try not to talk too much. He asked if Emmett brought the magazines. She said they were supposed to be her treat. He asked out of curiosity if Emmett could read. Crystal said she wasn't sure, but believed he only looked at the pictures. What was it Virgil called him that time, years ago? A bozo.

He said to Crystal, "What you want to do is pay close attention. Then later on you can tell what happened here as the star witness and get your name in the paper. I bet even your picture."

"I hadn't thought of that," Crystal said. "You really think so?"

They heard the car beep twice as it passed the house. Ready?

Carl was, in the chair facing the magazine table where the only lamp in the room was lit. Crystal stood smoking a cigaret, smoking three or four since drinking the orange juice glass of gin to settle her down. Light from the kitchen, behind her, showed her figure in the kimono she was wearing. Crystal looked fine to Carl.

But not to Emmett Long. Not the way he came in with magazines under his arm and barely paused before saying to her, "What's wrong?"

"Nothing," Crystal said. "Em, I want you to meet Carl, from home." Emmett staring at him now as Crystal said he was a busboy at Purity the same time she was working there. "And our moms are both Eastern Star."

"You're Emmett," Carl said, sounding like a salesman. "Glad to know you." Carl looking at a face from seven years ago, the same dead-eyed stare beneath the hat brim. He watched Emmett Long carry his magazines to the table, drop them on top of the ones there and glance over at Crystal. Carl watched him plant both hands on the table now, hunched over, taking time to what, rest? Uh-unh, decide how to get rid of this busboy so he could take Crystal to bed, Carl imagining Emmett doing it to her with his hat still on . . . And remembered his dad saying, "You know why I caught the Mauser round that time, the Spanish sniper picking me off? I was thinking instead of paying attention, doing my job."

Carl asked himself what he was waiting for. He said, "Emmett, bring out your pistol and lay it there on the table."

Crystal Lee Davidson knew how to tell it. She had recited her story enough times to marshals and various law enforcement people. This afternoon she was describing the scene to newspaper reporters— and the one from the **Oklahoman,** the Oklahoma City paper, kept interrupting, asking questions that were a lot different than ones the marshals asked.

She referred to Deputy Marshal Webster as "Carl" and the one from the **Oklahoman** said, "Oh, you two are on intimate terms now? You don't mind he's just a kid? Has he visited you here at the hotel?" Crystal staying a few days at the Georgian in Henryetta. The other reporters in the room would tell the **Oklahoman** to keep quiet for Christ sake, anxious for Crystal to get to the gunplay.

"As I told you," Crystal said, "I was in the doorway to the kitchen. Emmett's over here to my left, and Carl's opposite him but sitting down, his legs stretched out in his cowboy boots. I couldn't believe how calm he was."

"What'd you have on, dear?"

The **Oklahoman** interrupting again, some of the other reporters groaning.

"I had on a pink and red kimona Em got me at Kerr's in Oklahoma City. I had to wear it whenever he came."

"You have anything on under it?"

Crystal said, "None of your beeswax."

The **Oklahoman** said his readers had a right to know such details of how a gun moll dressed. This time the other reporters were quiet, like they wouldn't mind hearing such details themselves, until Crystal said, "If this big mouth opens his trap one more time I'm through and y'all can leave." She said, "Now where was I?"

"Emmett was leaning on the table."

"Sort of hunched over it," Crystal said. "He

looked over at me like he was gonna say something, and right then Carl said, 'Emmett?' He said, 'Draw your pistol and lay it there on the table.'"

The reporters wrote it down in their notebooks and then waited as Crystal took a sip of iced tea.

"I told you Em had his back to Carl? Now I see him turn his face to his shoulder and say to him, 'Do I know you from someplace?' Maybe thinking of McAlester, Carl an ex-convict looking to earn the reward money. Em asks him, 'Have we met or not?' And Carl says, 'If I told you, I doubt you'd remember.' Then—this is where Carl says, 'Mr. Long, I'm a deputy United States marshal. I'll tell you one more time to lay your pistol on the table.'"

A reporter said, "Crystal, I know they did meet. I'm Tony Antonelli from the Okmulgee **Daily Times** and I wrote the story about it."

"What you're doing," Crystal said, "is holding up my getting to the good part." Messing up her train of thought, too.

"But the circumstances of how they met," Tony Antonelli said, "could have everything to do with this story."

"Would you **please**," Crystal said, "wait till I'm done?"

It gave her time to tell the next part: how Emmett had no choice but to draw his gun, this big pearl-handle automatic, from inside his coat and lay it on the edge of the table, right next to him. "Now as he turns around," Crystal said, starting to grin, "this surprised look came over his face. He sees Carl sitting there, not with a gun in his hand but **Photoplay** magazine. Emmett can't believe his eyes. He says, 'Jesus Christ, you don't have a gun?' Carl pats the side of his chest where his gun's holstered under his coat and says, 'Right here.' Then he says, 'Mr. Long, I want to be clear about this so you understand. If I have to pull my weapon I'll shoot to kill.'" Crystal said to the reporters, "In other words, the only time Carl Webster draws his gun it's to shoot somebody dead."

It had the reporters scribbling in their notebooks and making remarks to one another. Tony Antonelli, the one from the Okmulgee paper saying now, "Listen, will you? Seven years ago Emmett Long held up Deering's drugstore in town and Carl Webster was there. Only he was known as Carlos then, he was still a kid. He stood by and watched Emmett Long shoot and kill an Indian from the tribal police happened to come in the store, a man Carl Webster must've known." Tony Antonelli, a good-looking young man, said to Crystal, "I'm sorry to interrupt, but I think the drugstore shooting could've been on Carl Webster's mind."

Crystal said, "I can tell you something else about that."

But now voices were chiming in, commenting and asking questions about the Okmulgee reporter's views:

"Carl carried it with him all these years?"

"Did he remind Emmett Long of it?"

"You're saying the tribal cop was a friend of his?"

"Both from Okmulgee, Carl thinking of becoming a lawman?"

"Carl ever say he was out to get Emmett?"

"This story's bigger'n it looks."

Crystal said, "You want to hear something else happened? How Carl was eating an ice cream cone that time and what Em did?"

They sat on the porch sipping bourbon at the end of the day, insects out there singing in the dark. A lantern hung above Virgil's head so he could see to read the newspapers on his lap.

"Most of it seems to be what this little girl told."

"They made up some of it."

"Jesus, I hope so. You haven't been going out with her, have you?"

"I drove down, took Crystal to Purity a couple of times."

"She's a pretty little thing. Has a saucy look about her in the pictures, wearing that kimona."

"She smelled nice, too," Carl said.

Virgil turned his head to him. "I wouldn't tell Bob McMahon that. One of his marshals sniffing around a gun moll." He waited, but Carl let that one go. Virgil looked at the newspaper he was holding. "I don't recall you were ever a buddy of Junior Harjo's."

"I'd see him and say hi, that's all."

"This Tony Antonelli has you two practically blood brothers. What you did was avenge his death. They wonder if it might even be the reason you joined the marshals."

"Yeah, I read that," Carl said.

Virgil put the **Daily Times** down and slipped the **Oklahoman** out from under it. "But now the Oklahoma City paper says you shot Emmett Long 'cause he took your ice cream cone that time. They trying to be funny?"

"I guess," Carl said.

"They could make up a name for you, as smart-aleck newspapers do, start calling you Carl Webster, the Ice Cream Kid?"

"You think so?"

"I'm getting the idea you like the attention."

Virgil saying it with some concern and Carl giving him a shrug. Virgil picked up another paper from the pile. "Here they quote the little girl saying Emmett Long went for his gun and you shot him through the heart."

"I thought they have her saying, 'straight through the heart,'" Carl said. "I told her, they want to know what I pack, tell 'em you think it's a Colt thirty-eight with the front sight filed down . . ." He turned to see his old dad staring at him with a solemn expression. "I'm kidding with you. What Emmett did, he tried to bluff me. He looked toward Crystal and called her name thinking I'd look over. But I kept my eyes on him, knowing he'd pick up his gun. He came around with it and I shot him."

"As you told him you would," Virgil said. "Every one of the newspapers played it up, your saying, 'If I have to pull my weapon I shoot to kill.' You tell 'em that?"

"The only one I told was Emmett," Carl said. "It had to of been Crystal told the papers."

"Well, that little girl sure tooted your horn for you."

"She only told what happened."

"All she had to. It's the telling that did it, made you a famous lawman overnight. You think you can carry a load like that?"

"Why not?" Carl said, grinning at his dad, but starting to show himself.

It didn't surprise his old dad. Virgil picked up his glass of bourbon and raised it to his boy, saying, "God help us show-offs."

4

The first piece Tony Antonelli wrote for the Okmulgee **Daily Times,** about Italian immigrants working in Oklahoma coal mines, he used "Death in the Dark" as a title and "Anthony Marcel Antonelli" as his byline. The editor of the paper said, "Who do you think you are, Richard Harding Davis? Get rid of the Marcel and call yourself Tony."

Tony Antonelli loved the literary style of Harding Davis, the greatest journalist in the world. But every time he tried to dress up his stories with color, with interesting observations—the way Harding Davis did in "The Death of Rodriguez," about a Cuban insurgent standing before a Spanish firing squad with a cigaret in the corner of his mouth, "not arrogantly nor with bravado"—the editor would cross out entire passages, saying, "Our readers don't give a rat's ass about what you think. They want facts."

About his interview with Crystal Davidson the

editor said, "Did Carl Webster ever tell you he was avenging the death of that tribal cop?"

"I only said they knew each other."

"You mean alleged to have known each other."

"And maybe," Tony said, "it gave Carl a motive, made it easier for him to shoot the bank robber."

"You're saying he needed a personal reason to gun down a wanted criminal?"

"What I meant, his knowing Junior might've enkindled a determination to do it."

"Did Carl Webster tell you directly that if he pulled his gun he'd shoot to kill?"

"It was something he told Crystal."

"And you accepted the word of a gun moll?"

Tony started looking for another writing job.

He was born in Krebs in 1903, the heart of Oklahoma coal mine country, the son of a coal miner, the reason he wrote about the hazards of working underground, the high incidence of deaths, the mine operators' reluctance to accept safety standards. And the editor chopped the drama out of his stories, telling Tony to get rid of "gasping for breath in a grotto of coal." He wrote about the Black Hand extorting money from Italian businesses, and the editor asked if he knew for a fact the Black Hand was related to the Mafia. He wrote about Italians in general not trusting banks and hiding their savings. "As much as fifty thousand dollars in small amounts buried in the backyards and vegetable gardens of Krebs, McAlester, Wilburton and other communities." He wrote that John Tua, the most influential Italian in Oklahoma, the **padrone** of the Antonellis and all the Italians working in the mines, often sat at night in his restaurant with twenty thousand dollars or more in the drawer of his desk, as much as a quarter of a million in his bank.

The editor said, "Where'd you get your figures? Some other Italian tell you?"

"Everyone knows it," Tony said. "Mr. Tua is a great man, dedicated to the welfare of immigrants. He gives people advice, finds them work, exchanges foreign currency. Why he keeps all that money."

The editor said, "I don't care for the one about the Klan, either. Who says they're out to get you people?"

"They hate Catholics," Tony said. "They believe we're no better than Negroes. And almost all Italians are Catholic. Even the fallen-away ones get married in the Church and have their babies baptized."

Tony wrote a story about the happy Fassino family's popular macaroni factory. Another one about a social club, the Christopher Columbus Society and its twenty-five-piece band that played at festivals and on the Fourth of July.

The editor said, "I think you're getting the hang of it. Now write one about the tendency of your people to overindulge in Choctaw beer and home-made wine."

That did it. Tony Antonelli quit the Okmulgee **Daily Times**. Within a few months he was living in Tulsa and writing for **True Detective Mystery** magazine. Finally, where he belonged.

They'd pay him two cents a word to start. He leafed through one of the latest issues to read a story that opened with "Light beams, sweeping the sky like flowing yellow ribbons against a backdrop of black, shone from the walls of the Colorado State Penitentiary one winter night in 1932."

He couldn't wait to start writing.

Two cents a word even for an "As Told To" story, a hundred bucks for five thousand words, nineteen and a half to twenty pages, and the opportunity of working up to a nickel a word. He'd found out they counted the pages, not the words. He believed he was meant to write for **True Detective,** be able to use more dialogue, the way people actually spoke. Here, the girl saying, "'I thought you were being hurt. Those screams,' she stammered." The response, "'I made them good, eh?' asked the imperturbable diver." Tony turned pages in the magazine and stopped at a photograph with the caption, "The laundry of Lee Hoey, wither the diver started on a peaceful errand, became the center of a strange conflict." The writer making even a caption work.

The editor of the Okmulgee paper, his problem, he wouldn't know good writing if John Barrymore read it to him.

Tony had written to **True Detective**'s editorial offices on Broadway in New York City, gave them samples of his original, unedited work and they called him. This editor said he liked the Black Hand piece and might run it if Tony could expand on the Mafia connection, their scheme to preside over all organized crime in America. Tony said he didn't see why not.

And then suggested, how about a close study of a deputy U.S. marshal, a good-looking young guy who was on his way to becoming the most famous lawman in America. The hot kid of the Marshals Service who said if he had to draw his gun, he would shoot to kill the wanted felon he was apprehending. "And Carl Webster has drawn his Colt .38 four times so far in his career. You can tell he's sharp just by the way he wears his panama, his suit's always pressed. You look at him and wonder where he keeps his gun."

"He's good-looking, uh?"

"Could be a movie star. You may remember him shooting Emmett Long four years ago? That was only his second. I'm getting details of the times he shot to kill. They were both in the papers. I might mention Carl is something of a ladies' man. He's been seen now and then with Emmett Long's gun moll, Crystal Davidson. He's younger than Crystal, still only twenty-five or six. His dad was on the **Maine** when she blew up in Havana harbor, and survived. The dad adds color, a touch of patriotism. What I want to do," Tony said, "is follow Carl while he tracks wanted criminals and write about what he thinks and feels, tap into his emotions and come up with the story of a True American Lawman: Carl Webster. His picture on the cover." Tony paused. "Drawing his Colt revolver."

The editor in his office on Broadway said it didn't sound too bad, but then wanted to know, "What else you got?"

Tony said, "How about the son of a millionaire who robs banks? Jack Belmont, out to make a name for himself. His dad's Oris Belmont of NMD Gas & Oil, worth a good twenty million, into refineries, car lots, has a tank farm. He occupies an entire floor of the Exchange National Bank building here in Tulsa."

He was giving this editor hard facts, confident he could write for **True Detective**.

"Jack Belmont's a young dude. Must have a dozen suits and pairs of shoes."

"How come I've never heard of him?"

"You will. Carl Webster's after him."

"If his daddy's rich, why's the kid rob banks?"

"That's what the story's about. Why did his old man cut him off? What was he up to? Outside of blowing up one of his dad's oil storage tanks. This guy's gonna pull something big before he's through."

"How do you get to him?"

"I told you, I follow Carl Webster."

There was a pause on the line before the editor in New York said, "You know who's the big news now, Pretty Boy Floyd."

Bingo.

Tony said in the same quiet voice he'd been using, "How would you like a profile of his girlfriend, Louly Brown? I understand she's hot stuff."

"Yeah? You know her?"

"I'm meeting her at the Mayo Hotel this coming week," Tony said, "for an interview."

There was another pause on the line.

"Which one you want to do first?"

"In a way," Tony said, "they're all related. When Louly Brown shot one of the guys in Pretty Boy's gang, guess who was there?" Tony paused a moment before saying, "Carl Webster."

5

In 1918, when Louly Brown was six years old, her dad, a Tulsa stockyard hand, joined the U.S. Marines and was killed at Bois de Belleau during the Great War. Her mom, Sylvia, sniffling as she held the letter from his lieutenant, told Louly it was a woods over in France.

In 1920 Sylvia married a hardshell Baptist by the name of Ed Hagenlocker and they went to live on his cotton farm near Sallisaw, below Tulsa on the south edge of the Cookson Hills. By the time Louly was twelve, Sylvia had two sons by Mr. Hagenlocker and the man had Louly out in the fields picking cotton. He was the only person in the world who called her by her Christian name, Louise. She hated picking cotton but Sylvia wouldn't say anything to Mr. Hagenlocker. Louly always thought of him that way, as Mr. Hagenlocker, and her mom as Sylvia, someone she never felt close to again. Mr. Hagenlocker believed that when you were old enough to do a day's work, you worked. It meant Louly was finished with school by the sixth grade.

In 1924, the summer Louly was twelve, they attended her cousin Ruby's wedding in Sallisaw. Ruby was seventeen, the boy she married, Charley Floyd, twenty. Ruby was dark but pretty, showing some Cherokee blood on her mama's side. Ruby had nothing to say to Louly at the wedding, but Charley called her kiddo and would lay his hand on her head and muss her bobbed hair that was reddish from her mom. He told her she had the biggest brown eyes he had ever seen on a little girl.

Just the next year she began reading about Charles Arthur Floyd in the paper: how he and two others went up to St. Louis and robbed the Kroger Food payroll office of $11,500. They were caught in Sallisaw driving around in a brand-new Studebaker they'd bought in Fort Smith, Arkansas. The Kroger Food paymaster identified Charley saying, "That's him, the pretty boy with apple cheeks." Gradually the newspapers began referring to Charley Floyd as "Pretty Boy."

Louly remembered him from the wedding as cute, but kind of scary the way he grinned at you—not being sure what he was thinking. She bet he hated being called Pretty Boy. Looking at his picture she cut out of the paper Louly felt herself getting a crush on this famous outlaw.

In 1929, while he was still at Jeff City, the Missouri State Penitentiary, Ruby divorced him for neglect and married a man from Kansas. Louly thought it was terrible, Ruby betraying Charley like that.

"Ruby don't see him ever again going straight," Sylvia said. "She needs a husband the same as I did to ease the burdens of life, have a father for her little boy Dempsey." Named for the world's heavyweight boxing champ.

Now that Charley was divorced Louly wanted to write and sympathize but didn't know which of his names to use. She had heard his friends called him Choc, after his fondness for Choctaw beer, his favorite beverage when he was in his teens and roamed Oklahoma and Kansas with harvest crews.

Louly opened her letter "Dear Charley," and said she thought it was a shame Ruby divorcing him while he was still in prison, not having the nerve to wait till he was out. What she most wanted to know, "Do you remember me from your wedding?" She stuck in with the letter a picture of herself in a bathing suit, standing sideways and smiling over her shoulder at the camera. This way her full-size sixteen-year-old breasts were seen in profile.

Charley wrote back saying sure he remembered her, "the little girl with the big brown eyes." Saying, "I'm getting out in March and going to Kansas City to see what's doing. I have given your address to an inmate here by the name of Joe Young who we call Booger, being funny. He is from Okmulgee but has to do another year or so in this garbage can and would like to have a pen pal as pretty as you are."

Nuts. But then Joe Young wrote her a letter with a picture of himself showing him as a fairly good-looking boy with big ears and blondish hair. He said he kept her bathing-suit picture on the wall next to his rack so he'd look at it before going to sleep and dream of her all night.

Once they were exchanging letters she told him how much she hated picking cotton, dragging that duck sack along the rows all day in the heat and dust, her hands raw from pulling the bolls off the stalks, gloves after while not doing a bit of good. Joe said in his letter, "What are you a nigger slave? You don't like picking cotton leave there and run away. It is what I done."

Pretty soon he said in a letter, "I am getting my release sometime next summer. Why don't you plan on meeting me so we can get together." Louly said she was dying to visit Kansas City and St. Louis, wondering if she would ever see Charley Floyd again. She asked Joe why he was in prison and he wrote back to say, "Honey, I am a bank robber, same as Choc."

It seemed like every week there'd be a story about Charley robbing another bank and his picture in the paper. It was exciting just trying to keep track of him, Louly getting chills and thrills knowing everybody in the world was reading about this famous outlaw who liked her brown eyes and had mussed her hair when she was a kid.

Joe Young wrote to say, "I am getting my release the end of August. I will let you know soon where to meet me."

Louly had been working winters at Harkrider's grocery store in Sallisaw for six dollars a week. She had to give five of it to her stepfather, Mr. Hagenlocker, the man never once thanking her—leaving a dollar to put in her running-away kitty. Working at the store from fall through winter, most of six months, she hadn't saved a whole lot but she knew she was leaving. She might have timid-soul Sylvia's looks, the reddish hair, but had the nerve and get-up-and-go of her daddy, killed in action charging a German machine gun nest in that woods in France.

Late in October, who walked in the grocery store but Joe Young. Louly knew him even wearing a suit, and he knew her, grinning as he came up to the counter, his shirt wide open at the neck. He said, "Well, I'm out."

She said, "You been out two months, haven't you?"

He said, "I been robbing banks. Me and Choc."

She thought she had to go to the bathroom, the

urge coming over her in her groin and then gone, Louly took a few moments to compose herself and act like the mention of Choc didn't mean anything special, Joe Young's grin in her face, giving her the feeling he was dumb as dirt. Some other convict must've wrote his letters for him. She said in a casual way, "Oh, is Charley here with you?"

"He's around," Joe Young said, acting shifty, like he was being watched. "Come on, we gotta go."

"I'm not ready just yet," Louly said. "I don't have my running-away money with me."

"How much you save?"

"Thirty-eight dollars.

"Jesus, working here two years?"

"I told you, Mr. Hagenlocker takes almost all my wages."

"You want, I'll crack his head for him."

"I wouldn't mind. The thing is, I'm not leaving without my money."

Joe Young looked at the door as he put his hand in his pocket saying, "Little girl, I'm paying your way. You won't need the thirty-eight dollars."

Little girl—she stood a good two inches taller than Joe Young, even in his run-down cowboy boots. She was shaking her head now. "Mr. Hagenlocker bought a Model A Roadster with my money, paying it off twenty a month."

"You want to steal his car?"

"It's mine, ain't it, if he's using my money?"

Louly had made up her mind and Joe Young was anxious to get out of here. She had pay coming, so they'd meet November 2 at the Georgian Hotel in Henryetta, around noon.

The day before she was to leave Louly told Sylvia she was sick. Instead of going to work she got her things ready and used the curling iron on her hair. The next day, while Sylvia was hanging wash, the two boys at school, and Mr. Hagenlocker was out on his tractor, Louly rolled the Ford Roadster out of the shed and drove into Sallisaw to get a pack of Lucky Strikes for the trip. She loved to smoke and had been doing it with boys but never had to buy the cigarets. When boys wanted to take her in the woods she'd ask, "You have Luckies? A whole pack?" It didn't cross her mind she was doing it for fifteen cents.

The druggist's son, one of her boyfriends, gave her a pack free of charge and asked where she was yesterday, acting sly, saying, "You're always talking about Pretty Boy Floyd, I wonder if he stopped by your house."

They liked to kid her about Pretty Boy. Louly, not paying much attention, said, "I'll let you know when he does." Then saw the boy about to spring something on her.

"The reason I ask, he was here in town yesterday, Pretty Boy was."

She said, "Oh?" careful now. The boy took his time and it was hard to keep herself from shaking him.

"Yeah, his family came down from Akins, his mama, two of his sisters, some others, so they could watch him rob the bank. He had a tommy gun, but didn't shoot anybody. Come out of the bank with two thousand five hundred and thirty-one dollars, him and two others. Gave some of the money to his people and they say to anybody he thought hadn't et in a while, everybody grinning at him."

This was the second time now he had been close by: first when his daddy was killed only seven miles away and now right here in Sallisaw, all kinds of people seeing him, damn it, but her. Just yesterday . . .

She had to wonder if she **had** been here would he of recognized her, and bet he would've.

She said to her boyfriend in the drugstore, "Charley ever hears you called him Pretty Boy, he'll come in for a pack of Luckies, what he always smokes, and shoot you through the heart."

The Georgian was the biggest hotel Louly had ever seen. Coming up on it in the Model A she was thinking these bank robbers knew how to live high on the hog. She pulled in front and a colored man in a green uniform coat with gold buttons and a peaked cap came around to open her door—and saw Joe Young on the sidewalk waving the doorman away, saying as he got in the car, "Jesus Christ, you stole it, didn't you? Jesus, how old are you, going around stealing cars?"

Louly said, "How old you have to be?"

He told her to keep straight ahead.

She said, "You aren't staying at the hotel?"

"I'm at a tourist court."

"Charley there?"

"He's around someplace."

"Well, he was in Sallisaw yesterday," Louly sounding mad now, "if that's what you call **around,**" seeing by Joe Young's expression she was telling him something he didn't know. "I thought you were in his gang."

"He's got an old boy name of Birdwell with him. I hook up with Choc when I feel like it."

She was almost positive Joe Young was lying to her.

"Am I gonna see Charley or not?"

"He'll be back, don't worry your head about it." He said, "We got this car, I won't have to steal one." Joe Young was in a good mood now. "What we need Choc for?" Grinning at her close by in the car. "We got each other."

It told her what to expect.

Once they got to the tourist court and were in No. 7, like a little one-room frame house that needed paint, Joe Young took off his coat and she saw the Colt automatic with a pearl grip stuck in his pants. He laid it on the dresser by a full quart of whiskey and two glasses and poured them each a drink, his bigger than hers. She stood watching till he told her to take off her coat and when she did told her to take off her dress. Now she was in her white brassiere and underpants. Joe Young looked her over before handing the smaller drink to her and clinking glasses.

"To our future."

Louly said, "Doing what?" Seeing the fun in his eyes.

He put his glass on the dresser, brought two .38 revolvers from the drawer and offered her one. She took it, big and heavy in her hand and said, "Yeah . . . ?"

"You know how to steal a car, and I admire that. But I bet you never held up a place with a gun."

"That's what we're gonna do?"

"Start with a filling station and work you up to a bank." He said, "I bet you never been to bed with a grown man, either."

Louly felt like telling him she was bigger than he was, taller, anyway, but didn't. This was a new experience, different than with boys her age in the woods, and she wanted to see what it was like.

Well, he grunted a lot and was rough, breathed

hard through his nose and smelled of Lucky Tiger hair tonic, but it wasn't that much different than with boys. She got to liking it before he was finished and patted his back with her rough, cotton-picking fingers till he began to breathe easy again. Once he rolled off her she got her douche bag out of Mr. Hagenlocker's grip she'd taken and went in the bathroom, Joe Young's voice following her with, "Whoooeee . . ." Then saying, "You know what you are now, little girl? You're what's called a gun moll."

Joe Young slept a while, woke up still snockered and wanted to get something to eat. So they went to Purity, Joe said was the best place in Henryetta.

Louly said at the table, "Charley Floyd came in here one time and everybody stayed in their house."

"How you know that?"

"I know everything about him was ever written, some things only told."

"Who was it named him Pretty Boy?"

"I found out it wasn't that paymaster in St. Louis, it was a woman named Beulah Ash. She ran the boardinghouse in Kansas City where Charley stayed."

Joe Young picked up his coffee he'd poured a shot into. He said, "You're gonna start reading about me, chile."

It reminded her she didn't know how old Joe Young was and took this opportunity to ask him.

"I'm thirty next month, born on Christmas Day, same as Baby Jesus."

Louly laughed out loud. She couldn't help it, seeing Joe Young lying in a feed trough with Baby Jesus, the three Wise Men looking at him funny. She asked Joe how many times he'd had his picture in the paper.

"When I got sent to Jeff City they was all kinds of pictures of me. Some I'm handcuffed."

She watched him sit back as the waitress came with their supper and he gave her a pat on the butt when she turned from the table. The waitress said, "Fresh," and acted surprised in a cute way. Louly was ready to tell how Charley Floyd had his picture in the Sallisaw paper fifty-one times in the past year, once for each of the fifty-one banks robbed in Oklahoma, all of them claiming Charley as the one who robbed them. But she knew it couldn't be true, so didn't mention it.

They finished their supper, breaded pork chops, and Joe Young told her to pay the bill—a buck-sixty for everything including rhubarb pie for dessert—out of her running-away money. They got back to the tourist court and he screwed her again on her full stomach, breathing through his nose, and she saw how this being a gun moll wasn't all a bed of roses.

In the morning they set out east on Highway 40 for the Cookson Hills, Joe Young driving the Model A with his elbow out the window, Louly holding her coat close to her, the collar up against the wind, Joe Young talking a lot, saying they'd go on up to Muskogee and hold up a filling station along the way. Show her how it was done.

Heading out of Henryetta she said, "There's one."

He said, "Too many cars."

Thirty miles later leaving Checotah, turning north toward Muskogee, Louly looked back and said, "What's wrong with that Texaco station?"

"Something about it I don't like," Joe Young said. "You have to have a feel for this work."

Louly said, "You pick it." She had the .38 he gave her in a black and pink bag Sylvia had crocheted for her.

They came up on Summit and crept through town, both of them looking, Louly waiting for him to choose a place to rob. She was getting excited. They came to the other end of town and Joe Young said, "There's our place. We can fill up, get a cup of coffee."

Louly said, "Hold it up?"

"Look it over."

"It's sure a dump."

Two gas pumps in front of a rickety place, paint peeling, a sign that said EATS and told that soup was a dime and a hamburger five cents.

They went in while a bent-over old man filled their tank, Joe Young bringing his whiskey bottle with him, almost drained now, and put it on the counter. The woman behind it was frail, flat-chested and appeared worn out, brushing strands of hair from her face. She placed cups in front of them and Joe Young poured what was left of the whiskey into his.

Louly did not want to rob this woman.

The woman saying, "I think she's dry," meaning his bottle.

Joe Young was concentrating on dripping the last drops into his cup. He said, "Can you help me out?"

Now the woman was pouring their coffee. "You want shine? Or I can give you Canadian whiskey for three dollars."

"Gimme a couple," Joe Young said, drawing his Colt to lay it on the counter, "and what's in the till."

Louly did not want to rob this woman. She was thinking you didn't **have** to rob a person just 'cause the person had money, did you?

The woman said, "Goddamn you, Mister."

Joe Young picked up his gun and went around to open the cash register. Taking out bills he said to the woman, "Where you keep the whiskey money?"

She said, "In there," despair in her voice.

He said, "Fourteen dollars?" holding it up, and turned to Louly. "Put your gun on her so she don't move. The geezer come in, put it on him, too." Joe Young went through a doorway to what looked like a kitchen.

The woman said to Louly, pointing the gun from the crocheted bag at her now, "How come you're with that trash? You seem like a girl from a nice family, have a pretty bag . . . There something wrong with you? My Lord, you can't do better'n him?"

Louly said, "You know who's a good friend of mine? Charley Floyd, if you know who I mean. He married my cousin Ruby." The woman shook her head and Louly said, "Pretty Boy Floyd," and wanted to bite her tongue.

Now the woman seemed to smile, showing black lines between the teeth she had. "He come in here one time. I fixed him breakfast and he paid me two dollars for it. You ever hear of that? I charge twenty-five cents for two eggs, four strips of bacon, toast and all you want of coffee, and he give me two dollars."

They got the fourteen from the till and fifty-seven dollars in whiskey money from the kitchen, Joe Young talking again heading for Muskogee, telling Louly it was something told him to go in there. How was this place doing business, two big gas stations only a few blocks away? So he'd brought the bottle in, see what it would get him. "You hear what she said? 'Goddamn you,' but called me 'Mister.'"

"Charley had breakfast in there one time," Louly said, "and paid her two dollars for it."

"Showing off," Joe Young said.

He decided they'd stay in Muskogee instead of crossing the Arkansas River and heading south.

Louly said, "Yeah, we must've come a good fifty miles today."

Joe Young told her not to get smart with him. "I'm gonna put you in a tourist cabin and see some boys I know. Find out where Choc's at."

She didn't believe him, but what was the sense of arguing?

It was early evening now, the sun almost gone.

The man who knocked on the door—she could see him through the glass part—was tall and slim in a dark suit, a young guy dressed up wearing a panama hat. She believed he was the police, but had no reason, standing here looking at him, not to open the door.

He said, "Miss," touched the brim of his

panama and showed her his I.D. and a star in a circle in a wallet he held open, "I'm Deputy U.S. Marshal Carl Webster. Who am I speaking to, please?"

She said, "I'm Louly Brown?"

He smiled straight teeth at her and said, "You're a cousin of Pretty Boy Floyd's wife Ruby, aren't you?"

Like getting ice-cold water thrown in her face she was so surprised. "How'd you know that?"

"We been talking to everybody he knows. You recall the last time you saw him?"

"At their wedding, eight years ago."

"No time since? How about the other day in Sallisaw?"

"I never saw him. But listen, him and Ruby are divorced."

The marshal, Carl Webster, shook his head. "He went up to Coffeyville and got her back. But aren't you missing a motor car, a Model A Roadster?"

She had not heard a **word** about Charley and Ruby being back together. Louly said, "The car isn't missing, a friend of mine's using it."

He said, "The car's in your name?" and recited the Oklahoma license number.

"I paid for it out of my wages. It just happens to be in my stepfather's name, Mr. Ed Hagenlocker."

"I guess there's some kind of misunderstanding," Carl Webster said. "Mr. Hagenlocker claims

it was stolen off his property in Sequoyah County.
Who's your friend borrowed it?"

She did hesitate before saying Joe Young.

"When's Joe coming back?"

"Later on. 'Cept he'll stay with his friends he
gets too drunk."

Carl Webster said, "I wouldn't mind talking to
him," and gave Louly a business card from his
pocket with a star on it and letters she could feel.
"Ask Joe to give me a call later on, or sometime
tomorrow if he doesn't come home. Y'all just driving around?"

"Seeing the sights."

Every time he caught her looking at him he'd
start to smile. Carl Webster. She could feel his name
under her thumb. She liked the way he shook her
hand and thanked her, and the way he touched his
hat, so polite for a U.S. marshal.

Joe Young returned about 9 A.M. making awful
faces working his mouth, trying to get a taste out
of it. He came in the room and took a good pull on
the whiskey bottle, then another, sucked in his
breath and let it out and seemed better. He said, "I
don't believe what we got into with those chickens
last night."

"Wait," Louly said. She told him about the

marshal stopping by, and Joe Young became jittery and couldn't stand still, saying, "I ain't going back. I done ten years and swore to Jesus I ain't ever going back." Now he was looking out the window.

Louly was curious about what Joe and his buddies did to the chickens, but knew they had to get out of here. She tried to tell him they had to leave, **right now.**

He was still drunk or starting over, saying now, "They come after me they's gonna be a shoot-out. I'm taking some of the scudders with me." Maybe not even knowing he was playing Jimmy Cagney now.

Louly said, "You only stole seventy-one dollars."

"I done other things in the State of Oklahoma," Joe Young said. "They take me alive I'm facing fifteen to life. I swear I ain't going back."

What was going **on** here? They're driving around looking for Charley Floyd—the next thing this dumbbell wants to shoot it out with the law and here she was in this room with him.

"They don't want **me**," Louly said. Knowing she couldn't talk to him, the state he was in. She had to get out of here, open the door and run. She got her crocheted bag from the dresser, started for the door and was stopped by the bullhorn.

The electrified voice loud, saying, "JOE YOUNG, COME OUT WITH YOUR HANDS IN THE AIR."

What Joe Young did—he held his Colt straight out in front of him and started firing through the glass pane in the door. Drunk. People outside returned fire, blew out the window, gouged the door with gunfire, Louly dropping to the floor with her bag, until she heard a voice on the bullhorn call out, "HOLD YOUR FIRE."

Louly looked up to see Joe Young standing by the bed with a gun in each hand now, the Colt and a .38. She said, "Joe, you have to give yourself up. They're gonna kill both of us you keep shooting." He reminded her again of James Cagney acting mad, in the movie where he squashes the grapefruit in the girl's face.

Joe Young didn't even look at her. He yelled out, "Come and get me!" and started shooting again, both guns at the same time. He stopped long enough to say to Louly, "I die, I'm gonna die game."

Louly's hand went in the crocheted bag and came out with the .38 he'd given her to help him rob places. From the floor, up on her elbows, she aimed the revolver at Joe Young, cocked it and **bam**, shot him through the chest.

Louly stepped away from the door and the marshal, Carl Webster, came in holding a revolver. She saw lawmen standing out in the road, some with rifles. Carl Webster was looking at Joe Young curled up on the floor. He holstered his revolver, took the .38 from Louly and sniffed the barrel and stared at her without saying anything before going to one knee to see if Joe Young had a pulse. He got up saying, "The Oklahoma Bankers Association wants people like Joe dead, and that's what he is. They're gonna give you a five-hundred dollar reward for killing your friend."

"He wasn't a friend."

"He was yesterday. Make up your mind."

"He stole the car and made me go with him."

"Against your will," Carl Webster said. "Stay with that you won't go to jail."

"It's true, Carl," Louly said, showing him her big brown eyes with soul in them. "Really."

The headline in the Tulsa **World,** over a small photo of Louise Brown, said SALLISAW GIRL SHOOTS ABUDUCTOR.

According to Louise, she had to stop Joe Young or be killed in the exchange of gunfire. She also said her name was Louly, not Louise. The marshal on the scene said it was a courageous act, the girl shooting her abductor. "We considered Joe Young a mad-dog felon with nothing to lose." The marshal said that Joe Young was suspected of being a member of Pretty Boy Floyd's gang. He also mentioned that Louly Brown was related to Floyd's wife and acquainted with the desperado.

The headline in the Tulsa paper, over a larger photo of Louly, said GIRL SHOOTS PRETTY BOY FLOYD GANG MEMBER. The story told that Louly Brown was a friend of Pretty Boy's and had been abducted by the former gang member who, according to Louly, "was jealous of Pretty Boy and kidnapped me to get back at him."

By the time the story had appeared everywhere from Fort Smith, Arkansas, to Toledo, Ohio, the most popular headline was GIRLFRIEND OF PRETTY BOY GUNS DOWN MAD-DOG FELON.

The marshal, Carl Webster, came to Sallisaw on business and stopped in Harkrider's for a pack of cigarets and a sack of Beechnut scrap. He was surprised to see Louly.

"You're still working here?"

"No, Carl, I'm shopping for my mom. I got my reward money and I'll be leaving here pretty soon. Mr. Hagenlocker hasn't said a word to me since I got home. He's afraid I might shoot him."

"Where you going?"

"This writer for **True Detective** wants me to come to Tulsa. They're willing to put me up at the Mayo Hotel and pay a hundred dollars for my story. Reporters from Kansas City and St. Louis, Missouri, have already been to the house."

"You're sure getting a lot of mileage out of knowing Pretty Boy, aren't you?"

"They start out asking about my shooting that dumbbell Joe Young, but what they really want to know, if I'm Charley's girlfriend. I say, 'Where in the world did you get that idea?'"

"You don't deny it."

"I say, 'Believe what you want, since I can't change your mind.' All I'm doing is having some fun with them."

"And becoming famous," Carl said. "Maybe it can get you something you've thought of doing."

"Like what, become a chorus girl? Yeah, I'll get a job in **George White's Scandals.**" Louly picked up her sack of groceries.

Carl took it from her and they walked out of the store to her Ford roadster parked on the street, Carl saying, "I wouldn't be surprised you can do just about anything you want. You still have my card?"

"I keep it in my Bible," Louly said.

Carl, holding the sack of groceries, smiled at this farm girl who'd shot a wanted fugitive and entertained herself talking to newspaper reporters. The photos of her didn't show her hair's blaze of color, or the easy way she could look up at you with those brown eyes. Or the way she said to him now, "I like your hat."

Carl couldn't help smiling. He said, "Give me a call when you get to Tulsa, I'll buy you an ice cream soda."

6

The reason Tony Antonelli was on hand to write what he was thinking of calling "The Bloody Bald Mountain War," he had returned to Krebs on his own to cover a labor strike.

The mine operators announced they were cutting wages by 25 percent, and the miners of Local 2327 walked out of Osage No. 5. Their demand: the company continue to pay them a flat six dollars and ten cents a day. Tony had grown up with most of the Italian miners and wanted to hear their side of the disagreement. They told him they were standing for a bare-minimum living wage, nothing less. It was bad enough, they said, spending ten hours in the hole with those stinking mules. They said the animals stunk so bad of putrid gas, you could blow yourself to hell striking a spark with your pick. Tony wasn't sure if this was true but wrote it anyway. It was good stuff, the attitude of the miners.

The company brought in strikebreakers along with a man by the name of Nestor Lott, at one time a special agent for the Justice Department in

Georgia, going after moonshiners defying Prohibition by the unlawful manufacture and sale of alcohol. The Krebs chief of police, a man named Fausto Bassi, told Tony that Nestor Lott was known to have gunned down more moonshiners than he arrested, and that the man's judgment had a "hair-trigger."

Nestor Lott wore two .45 automatics, military issue, one holstered on each hip and snugged to his legs with leather thongs. Tony wrote in his notebook: "He is a man of small stature, no more than five-three, who stares with a look of intensity in his cold gray eyes that holds one's attention. When he smiles, which is seldom, one is never certain if it is to express pleasure, or even goodwill, for the smile never shows in his eyes of steel."

Nestor Lott got rid of the company strikebreakers saying they were drunks and derelicts with no personal stake in the situation, and recruited members of the local Ku Klux Klan for the job. He told them, "You know these dagos are all Socialists, enemies of our American way. We run 'em out now or they'll be after your jobs, your farms, and they'll lure your Christian women as Eyetalians know how to do."

The next move of Nestor and his Klansmen, they put on their white robes and pointed hoods and drove out in their cars to a ridge overlooking the Osage No. 5 shaft and the strikers standing by the fence in front of the mine works with their signs. Nestor strung his shooters—each one armed with a rifle—along the high ground, all those white sheets flapping in the wind not much more than a hundred yards from the strikers squinting up at them. Next, he sent a Klansman to drive down there with a message, an ultimatum, fixed to the radiator of his car. It said in big letters:

YOU HAVE 5 MINUTES TO LEAVE
BEFORE WE OPEN FIRE

The miners never thought of leaving. They yelled at the bedsheets up on the ridge for the entire five minutes calling them dirty names, dirty laundry, and ran for their lives when the Klansmen fired a volley at them and kept firing and laughing and swearing, killing three and wounding seven before the strikers could bust through the fence to reach the cover of company structures.

The mine operators had a fit at how it would look, knowing the United Mine Workers would now slander the company in newspapers across the country. They paid the hospital bills of the wounded, gave the families of the ones killed a check for five hundred dollars, told the little two-gun weasel to go back to Georgia, and set up arbitration meetings with the union.

But Nestor Lott hung around, warmed up now,

restless, feeling confident about the Klan behind him. What caught his eye was the flow of prohibited wine, beer and liquor all over this county—the Oklahoma state prison sitting there at McAlester, only a few miles from Krebs. Nestor said to Tony Antonelli, taking notes in the café where Nestor was having his noon dinner, "You know the women sell that Choc beer out the back of wagons? In tubs of ice? I'm talking about Eyetalian women making money getting people drunk."

Tony felt heat on his face, the boob not realizing he was speaking to an Italian, or not caring. He closed his notebook and said to Nestor sure, he knew of women who brewed Choc. "They make it from barley, hops, throw in some tobacco and a few fishberries, but it hardly amounts to much alcohol. Miners drink it as a tonic for health reasons, water around mining camps being of poor quality, some of it even poisonous."

It didn't move Nestor. He said, "I know of bunco joints where you gamble your money away, no chance in hell of winning. Where you can get whores who'll give you their disease, and liquor that'll turn you blind. They bring it up from places like Old Mexico."

Tony said, "I never heard of any Italians in Krebs running hard liquor."

"But the chief of police's Eyetalian," Nestor

said. "Man name of Bassi, speaks with an accent I guarantee ain't American. What's he doing about all the liquor violations?" Nestor waited for an answer, his blunt stare bearing on Tony with suspicion. Later on Tony would open his notebook and try to describe the look, the accusing stare, everyone against this squirt upholding a law no one cared about.

Finally he spoke.

"You want to write a good story?"

Tony waited.

Nestor said, "You know that big roadhouse out by Bald Mountain? The other side of McAlester?"

Tony said, "Jack Belmont's place."

"That's the one," Nestor said. "I'm gonna ride in and hit it with my Christian Avengers. Burn it to the ground."

Tony said, "You think the police'll let you?"

Nestor said, "Boy, I don't need their permission."

The first thing Tony thought of doing, sitting behind the wheel in his car, about to turn on the ignition, was drive out to Belmont's roadhouse and tell him what was afoot. He knew for a fact there wasn't anything harmful about the whiskey. He wasn't sure about the girls, but they appeared healthy and fun-loving. A cutie out there named

Elodie had caught his eye. Yeah, what he should do, let Belmont know the two-gun weasel was coming on a raid.

But then something he'd been thinking about lately popped in his mind. People in the wilds studying animal behavior, how they'd watch a pride of lions, even give each one a name, and feel sorry for the runt cub, Jimmy, that never got any tit and they'd want to save its life, bring the runt into camp and give it nourishment. But they couldn't 'cause they'd be intruding on nature with their own behavior. They had to watch the daddy lion come along and eat Jimmy. Wasn't it the same thing here? These people living by their own rules of behavior?

In no time Jack Belmont's plight had become part of the metaphor Tony was working on, scribbling in his notebook, trying to draw a literary parallel between animal behavior and human behavior, as it played out in the wilds of eastern Oklahoma.

What occupied Jack Belmont's mind these days, outside of making money and becoming a famous outlaw, was Norm Dilworth's wife, Heidi.

Heidi Winston from Seminole.

Where Norm had taken her out of a whorehouse to the shack by the Kiefer rail yard. Where she was when he and Norm went to prison. Where she stayed doing washing for railroad hands till she got a job as a chambermaid—she said—at the St. James Hotel in Sapulpa. It turned out she was telling the truth, 'cause it was what she was doing when they came out of prison to rob banks with the Emmett Long gang. Jack and Norm would swing back to stay at the St. James till Emmett called about another job. It drove Jack crazy knowing she was in bed with Norm in the next room. He'd listen, holding an empty water glass to the wall, his ear pressed against it, and he'd hear their voices, sometimes her moans when they were doing it.

Heidi still kept giving him the eye. Or she'd bend over in front of him in a low-cut dress to pick out an olive from the dish on the coffee table and put it in her mouth looking at him and kind of suck on it. The time came the gang split up after a robbery and Jack got back to the hotel before Norm. He took Heidi by the arm into his room. Didn't say a word to her getting out of his pants, Heidi pulling her dress over her head, neither one speaking while he humped her on the bed as hard and fervently as he could to show how he felt about her. After, Heidi said, "I was beginning to wonder about you."

In some ways Jack Belmont was growing up. He could review his failures and sometimes admit the ones that didn't work were his own fault. Like blackmailing Oris. It was a good idea but done on the spur of the moment before working it out. The same with kidnapping Nancy Polis. He'd jumped the gun on that one, not realizing she might know who he was. Or then, not believing for a minute his own dad would have sent him to prison, Jesus, for blowing up that empty storage tank. It sure made a cloud.

What did he learn about robbing banks from Emmett Long? Go in and scare the shit out of everybody and walk out with the money. How else would you do it? Emmett Long showed he was too old for the outlaw life, letting that tricky marshal set him up and shoot him. Carl Webster. No, the only thing he learned from Emmett Long was if you wanted another man's wife, you'd likely have to shoot him to get her.

So what should he do about Norm Dilworth?

For a dumb guy Norm was smart in a countrified kind of way, hooking them up with bootleggers who put them in the speakeasy business in Krebs.

He didn't want to shoot Norm when he wasn't looking. He didn't want to call him out, either, Norm a dead shot with rifle or revolver. He'd already killed two cops chasing them out of Coalgate that time. Leaned out and drilled them through the windshield of the police car. The only person Jack had shot was the colored boy running from the mob during the race riot, when Jack was fifteen. It told him he ought to shoot somebody now that he was grown, get a feel for it.

He'd been thinking of having some boys snatch Nancy Polis from her boardinghouse, send Oris a ransom note for a hundred thousand or he'd never see her again, and hope his dad still loved her. Jack was also thinking of holding up the Exchange National Bank in Tulsa, where Oris was now on the board. Jack saw a meeting interrupted, the secretary running in to tell them Mr. Belmont's son had just robbed the bank downstairs.

It was an image in his mind Jack liked to play with.

But if you were a famous outlaw you'd have state and federal law after you, the Carl Websters wanting to shoot you down, and you'd have to have a place where you could lie low. That's why the speakeasy business coming along as a sideline was a good idea, even if it was Norm's.

It got them the café in Krebs they turned into a speak, and later on the feed store off the highway, out of business, they bought and fixed up, added rooms out the back and upstairs with fifteen hundred of bank loot Heidi had saved out of Norm's cut. Now they had a roadhouse not far from a north-south highway that ran up through eastern Oklahoma.

Heidi said she'd always wanted to be a high-class madam. She got hold of three girls who worked in Seminole and one off the street in Krebs who'd run away from home and was too scared to go back and face her daddy. Heidi put her arm around the quivering girl and told her, "Honey, take my word, you have nothing to worry about. You're sitting on what every man I ever knew wants a piece of."

It meant Heidi would stay at the roadhouse with the girls, and Jack most of the time, while Norm ran the speak in Krebs. It was the kind of town Norm liked, full of miners coming out of the hole thirsty, but the streets not clogged with traffic stuck in mud like oil boom towns.

The roadhouse had cars lined up in front all night, but was fairly quiet during the day, giving Jack all the time he wanted with Heidi. It was a sweet deal.

Only he wished she wouldn't talk so much lying in bed naked. Always speaking as a madam about business. And always had the radio playing. Right now Rudy Vallee and his Connecticut Yankees doing "You're Driving Me Crazy." What Heidi was doing to Jack. Wanting to raise the girls' price from three to four dollars. Set it at more than half of a miner's daily wage, they wouldn't get so many of them in here.

"They're the business," Jack said.

Heidi told him there were whores in Krebs'd screw you for four bits. "Let 'em get laid in town and come out here to drink and play monte. You know what it's like to screw a coal miner, even after he's washed up? You get filthy dirty. You ever look at the laundry in the morning, the sheets? Coal miners are dirtier'n oil workers any day, and I'm talking about all kinds, roughnecks, drillers, tool dressers, tankies, tankies are the worst. Shooters, all they do is talk. Ask you how many mistakes you're allowed shooting nitro. The answer's none. The shooter's talking away while these other guys off the patch are waiting in the front room with their hard-ons."

"The girls complain about coal miners?"

"They won't dare say a word. They're clearing a buck and a half every time a guy drops his pants. What I'm telling you is how I feel about it."

Jack had got up as she was talking and put on his pants. Now he sat on the side of the bed with his shoes and socks, his back to Heidi.

"I can't imagine you working in a house."

"Stables are cleaner," she said.

Lying behind him full-length naked, tan arms and white white breasts. Nicer ones than he'd seen on any Tulsa whore. He'd bet Nancy Polis had nice ones. He saw old Oris slipping a hand into Nancy's dress.

"Why'd you stay there?"

"I'd try to run—Eugene'd have his guys he called his dogs out looking for me. I'd be dragged back, he'd put a leather glove on over his big mitt and beat my behind till it was raw. I told you, Norm saved my life. He said the only way he could come in that house again was with a gun. He told Eugene, 'You come after us I'll shoot you dead.' This was down in Seminole. We come up to Keifer, that house you were at, and it wasn't long before Eugene showed up, him and two others with guns. They busted in while Norm and I were in bed asleep."

Jack turned enough to look at her lying naked.

"Yeah . . . ?"

"Eugene had the drop on Norm. But we always kept this gun under the covers when we went to bed. Norm shot Eugene and about set the bed on fire."

"Shot him dead?"

"It come out his back and broke a window in the front room. I got the rifle and fired at the two running away but only hit one of 'em."

"What'd you do with the bodies?"

"Laid 'em across the railroad tracks."

"Norm never mentioned that to me."

"He isn't one to pat himself on the back."

"He never once mentioned ever shooting anybody."

Jack turned his head to look at her again, Heidi digging at her navel with a fingernail. She said, "That's Norm," without looking over.

"He was a good customer of yours?"

"Norm? He came two times. I got beat in between. Norm saw my raw heinie and the next time he came with the gun."

"You got married right away?"

"He asked me—what am I gonna say?"

Jack put his socks on and then his shoes, but didn't tie the laces or get up. He said, "What do we do about him?"

Heidi turned her head on the pillow to look at Jack, her finger still fooling with her navel.

"Aren't you getting what you want?"

"I don't like you being with him."

"He's my husband."

"That's what I mean."

She said, "You want us to get married?"

Jack bent down to tie his shoes. Ruth Etting was singing now on the radio, "Ten Cents a Dance."

"Let's see how it works out," Jack said.

"How what works out?"

"You and me. See how we get along."

"Lemme ask you again," Heidi said. "Aren't you getting what you want?"

Nestor Lott said, "In the movin' pitcher you see this fella name of Ben Cameron watching these white boys putting on bedsheets, dressing up like ghosts to scare some nigger kids. It gives Ben an idea and your great organization is born that day."

Here was Nestor addressing his Klansmen inside a rickety Pentacostal church on the outskirts of Krebs. Telling them about **The Birth of a Nation,** calling it one of the greatest moving pictures of all time, first appearing eighteen years ago, before Al Jolsen and talkies, and you could see it right now at the picture show in town.

"You want to know the truth about Reconstruction after the Civil War? What it was like? You want to see niggers terrorizing white families? Shoving white people off the sidewalk? Niggers in the state legislature with their bare feet up on their desks? Well, back then the Klan was all we had to fight nigger rule and Reconstruction. Do you know if they found white robes in your closet you could get shot? The Klan rode then to put the niggers back in their place. This time it's the Eyetalians making trouble, breaking the law, and this Eyetalian chief of police they got lets 'em get away with it." Nestor stopped. He frowned at his audience, something perplexing him. He said, "How come the worst troublemakers are all dark-complected? You notice that?" Yes, they did, the audience nodding. "I went to see this police chief by the name of"— Nestor dug a piece of notepaper from his coat pocket, folded it open and looked at it—"Fausto Bassi, I think it says here. I was gonna ask him what kind of American name was Fausto Bassi, but I didn't. I asked him if he knew who I was. And you know what he said to me?"

Bob McMahon had two marshals in his office, Carl Webster and Lester Crowe, who was in his late forties now, both sitting across the desk from their boss. Lester Crowe was the marshal who'd come out to the Webster place with McMahon, that time Carl shot the man stealing his cows some years ago.

"This fella walks in the police chief's office with two .45s hanging on him, a Justice badge pinned on his lapel. He says to Fausto Bassi, 'You know who I am?' Fausto's okay, he's smart but a little too easygoing, has a belly on him. He says, 'Yes, you're Nestor Lott. We have you down for a triple homicide and seven attempted, over at Osage Mining. Why don't you sit down while we wait for the judge to sign the warrants?' Just his woman clerk's in the office at the time. She says Nestor and this local fella with him pull their guns, Nestor both of his, and lock the chief and her in a jail cell, and they drive off. This was yesterday afternoon."

Lester Crowe said, "If the chief knows who he is, knows he's wanted and the man's standing there in his office—"

McMahon cut him off saying, "I guess he didn't think Nestor'd pull on him."

"I'd of arrested him he's walking in the door," Lester said. Lester was smoking a cigaret, tapping the ash in the cuff of his pants. He had told Carl one time it kept out the moths.

"I called Justice," McMahon said, "after the mine shooting to check on Nestor. I find out they're thinking of changing their name from the United States Bureau of Investigation to the Federal Bureau of Investigation, or, the FBI."

Lester said, "It should be the FB of I."

"It's their bureau," McMahon said, "they can call it what they want. That lint picker J. Edgar Hoover's still running it."

"I've seen him," Lester said. "He's a slick article but acts like he's got some old-woman in him."

"They called back this morning to say Nestor Lott's no longer an agent. They had trouble with him in Georgia, shooting moonshiners he didn't have to, and fired him. All you boys have to do is arrest him for impersonating a federal officer. But now I'm thinking once you get him, hand him over to the county prosecutor. I think shooting the miners will be enough to get him electrocuted. You won't have to fuss with him over wearing the badge."

Lester said, "He's hiding someplace?"

"He's raiding places that sell liquor," McMahon said. "Nestor and about fifty of his spooks, these Klansmen he calls his Christian Avengers. All Fausto and the cops can do is watch."

Lester said, "Well, if selling booze is against the law—"

"For Christ sake," McMahon said, "I want you to arrest the man and hand him over to the county. Can you do that without arguing about it?"

"I just want it clear in my mind," Lester said, "who's who." As they got up he said to Carl, "You can drive this trip. Put a Thompson in the trunk, case Nestor wants to make something of it."

Carl was aware of Bob McMahon watching them. He didn't say anything now and neither did Carl. Carl never had much to do with Lester Crowe but listen to him talk.

Bob says he don't want me arguing with him. Was I arguing? I said if this man Nestor Lott is closing down speakeasies he's upholding the law, isn't he?

Whether he's impersonating a federal officer or not. Am I right on that? You're damn tootin'."

Carl was falling asleep driving the two-door Chevrolet the hundred miles of farmland and hills thick with redbud trees, from Tulsa down to Krebs, listening to Lester talk.

"We're suppose to arrest this guy for pinning a badge on his chest while he's doing what his job was before the operators fired him and he had the coal miners shot? Bob seems to think he'll burn for it. Oh, is that right? How about leaving it to a court of law?"

Carl was wondering if he'd see Louly Brown again. If he'd be back in Tulsa while she was there for her interview.

"There's nothing simple about a marshal's job," Lester said. "Apprehend wanted fugitives. It sounds simple. But what's a fugitive? A person wanted by the law who flees or escapes. Has Nestor Lott run away? No, he's down there making raids on people breaking the law."

Carl was looking at Louly Brown in his mind, her red hair, thinking she wouldn't be too young for him if she was twenty. But she might still be in her teens. He had seen her date of birth but couldn't remember it now. He believed it was 1912.

Lester was telling Carl about Lake Okeechobee now, in Florida, where he was from originally, this giant lake thirty miles long and only six feet deep, like a huge saucer, alligators in it, and some of the finest bass fishing in the whole country.

"The hurricane of twenty-eight, a hunnert and fifty mile an hour wind blew the lake over the muck dike and killed eighteen hunnert and thirty-eight folks."

He said he was thinking of going back there.

Carl was still thinking of Louly Brown.

They came to Krebs and met with the chief of police in his office. The first thing Lester wanted to know, why in hell hadn't Fausto picked up Nestor and thrown him in jail.

"Because he has more men than I do," Fausto said. "All those bogeymen in bedsheets who enjoy shooting their guns."

Lester wanted to know what in hell the county sheriff was doing about the situation. "Some convicts ran away from a road gang," Fausto said, "and the sheriff is out with his dogs. His favorite thing."

Lester decided what they'd do. He'd stay in town with the Thompson, wait for Nestor to hit a speakeasy still open, here or some other coal town to the east. Carl'd go out to the roadhouse the chief told them about. Lester said, "Fella runs it use to be in the Emmett Long gang."

Carl didn't say anything.

7

The night before the raid on the roadhouse Nestor told his Avengers at the rickety church, "I want us to come at them out of the sun, first light shining hard on the window glass as we roll up on the place. They don't hear us, they're dead to the world from boozin' all night. They open their eyes to squint out the window, they don't even see us till we're spread across the front of the place. Twelve cars or more with .30-30s, a case of Austin Powder, caps, fuses, as I announce to them with the bullhorn, 'Come out with your hands in the air or get blown to hell. Bring your whores out into the light of day.' You set your torches afire and advance on the house."

These people loved their torches. They said you bet, that's how to do it, run the scalawags out of the county.

The next morning it was still dark when Nestor got to the church with his canteen of coffee laced with brandy, something he'd picked up in France during the war. It started him thinking of that time sixteen years ago, moving out of the village of

Bousheres to take the woods, and how he had to keep his men moving in the howl of German artillery splintering trees, pounding out shell holes to bury them under mounds of earth. His officers had said the French command were idiots, we'd never make it to the woods. Except the Frogs were running this side of the war and if they said take the woods, even if you might get your legs blown off or your voice burned out by mustard gas, you took your men to the woods. Nestor had stood in the open waving his big revolver, the Webley he'd taken off a dead British officer some time before, waved it screaming at his men to come on, keep moving, threatening to shoot anybody pretending to be hit or trying to hide. He did, too, shot three of them looking right at him, and the rest ran across the field, most to get mowed down by machine-gun fire. Nestor lost more men that summer than any platoon sergeant in the Seventh Infantry and was given a medal for valor.

He wore it this morning, his Distinguished Service Cross, pinned to the breast pocket of his suitcoat, below the bureau shield on his lapel, waiting from dawn till going on eight o'clock before all his Avengers had straggled in. The late ones saying well, shit, they had their chores, didn't they? Or their wife was sick or their dog got run over. Nestor finally had twelve cars here counting his De Soto, a couple of men in some, no more than four in the others, thirty-four Avengers all told.

Except now the sky was overcast, no way to come riding out of the sun. Shit. But as long as they were here, armed and ready, Nestor said, "Hell, let's get her done."

Carl Webster arrived the night before.

He walked in the roadhouse and up to Jack Belmont at the bar, only a few miners down the shiny length drinking.

"You having a slow night?"

It turned Jack around and he had to look toward the door to see who else was coming in. He recognized Carl Webster in his panama, couldn't be anyone else.

"You raiding the place by yourself?"

"I'm not the one does that," Carl said.

He let the ex-convict son of a multimillionaire stare at him not knowing what was going on. Like the girls at the table in kimonos and playsuits were staring with raised eyebrows, waiting. Carl recognized a couple of them from a house in Seminole and took time to touch the brim of his hat to them.

Jack Belmont was squinting now, trying to focus on what this marshal was doing here.

"Don't tell me—you came to try to arrest me."

"I wouldn't mind," Carl said, "but I haven't seen

your name on a warrant since Emmett Long passed on. You aren't a big enough name with the Marshals Service."

That caused Jack Belmont to have to think of something. He said, "Then you must've come in for a drink."

"I don't mind," Carl said.

He watched Jack Belmont motion to the bartender who brought a couple of shot glasses over and filled them up. Carl raised his and took a sip, gave Jack a nod and finished the shot. He said, "I don't raid stills or liquor joints, but you know a fella's been doing it around here. I imagine it's why you don't have too many customers this evening. Nobody wants to get shot over a glass of whiskey."

Jack said, "You're talking about Nestor Lott."

"That's the one. He comes by, I'll be here to put him in jail." He saw Jack Belmont frowning now. "For pretending he's a government agent," Carl said. "You aren't allowed to do that, even if you think it's for the national welfare. Stop men from getting drunk and beating up on their wives."

Jack said, "You want another?"

"I don't mind. He's got those Klan dimwits running around shooting people."

"You think he's coming here?"

"Sooner or later, seeing as you're in violation of the Volstead Act."

The bartender filled their glasses and Carl drank his.

Jack said, "You come here by yourself—you think you can stop him?"

"You're gonna help me," Carl said.

Jack watched this marshal in his dark suit and nifty panama roam the place looking out windows. Over at the table with the girls now, talking to them, acting like he knew Violet and Elodie. Jesus, he even knew Heidi, Heidi running up to him with a big grin. Now they were hugging each other like they were sweethearts. This marshal must've spent some time in Seminole at the whorehouse. Else he'd arrested them for prostitution, got to know them that way. But would they be glad to see him?

Carl Webster was not like any officer of the law Jack had ever met—with their official way of speaking, never smiling at anything you said was funny.

Now he was at the bar with Norm Dilworth having another drink, talking like they were pals. Talking about Emmett Long or prison most likely, the marshal knowing what Norm had been doing with his life. Jack stepped up to the bar to join them.

They were talking about guns.

Norm coming right out to tell him he had his

own Winchester, his favorite gun, a couple of revolvers, .38s, and a double-barrel scatter gun. Now he was saying Jack was the one had the guns.

Carl turned to him. "Is that right?"

Jack hesitated, a government cop asking him something like that.

But then Norm said, "Jack brought a few hunting rifles to pass around and a Thompson submachine gun he bought off a guard at the prison. Case some gang tries to take over the business. Come down from Kansas City or Chicago. I wish I'd had it when Nestor Lott raided my speak. He come in shooting, killed my bartender standing with his hands in the air. One of the miners yelled at him, said something in Italian, and he got shot too, for no reason. A whole crowd of KKKers come in wearing their bedsheets and got busy busting the place up, smashing bottles . . . But you know they took a few with 'em."

Carl said, "He didn't put you in jail?"

"I slipped out while they were busy."

Carl kept facing Norm. "How many men you have here?"

It irritated Jack. He said, "We got enough."

But now Norm was telling him two bartenders, two bouncers, a couple of colored boys, one of 'em cooks. "I never asked did they know how to shoot, the two being colored. The maids don't come till morning. With us three that's seven I know of can use a gun. And Heidi, that makes eight. I know my wife can shoot, I saw her."

"No kidding," Carl said, "you two are married?" Carl grinning at the hayseed. "You got a smart girl there's had a hard life."

Jesus Christ, now his grin irritated Jack. Talking about a whore like she was some sweet girl lived down the road. He said to Carl, "You must know Heidi pretty well."

"We've talked a couple of times."

Jack said, "After you screwed her?"

Carl stared at him without a trace of what he was thinking on his face. He said, "You can be a mean bugger, huh? Nobody pays attention to you."

"I'm talking about when she worked in a cat house," Jack said, "in Seminole." He turned to Norm saying, "I don't mean since you got married. You understand that, don't you?" Norm seemed to nod his head and Jack felt he was okay, being an honest Injun and said, "I mean, after all, she was a whore at that time, wasn't she?"

Carl said, "Norm, does he run this place?"

Jack looked at Norm.

Norm saying, "He acts like it. What I think he does mostly is sniff around Heidi. If he's what she wants, I don't need her no more. But she hasn't said nothing."

"That's not my business," Carl said. "You tell him what Nestor's like?"

"I sure did."

Jesus Christ—talking about him, Jack standing only a couple of feet away.

"What'd he say?"

"Said don't worry about it."

"Means he can handle Nestor?"

"Beats me."

Jack looking from Carl to Norm and back again.

Carl saying, "Why doesn't he want me to help him?"

"He's a spoiled kid," Norm said, "thinks he's smart. But hasn't had an idea yet for making money that's worked. I'm the one said let's get in the whiskey business."

"What do you stay with him for? Find an oil patch'll hire you and get a regular job. You know how this life ends."

"Dead or in the clink," Norm said. "I been thinking about drawing my cut, take Heidi out of here before she gets in trouble."

Jack's eyes moved from Norm as he mentioned Heidi to Carl.

Carl saying, "Where's the Thompson? You ever fire it?"

Norm shook his head.

"Get it, I'll show you how it works."

Norm said, "You want a drink first?"

Carl said, "I don't mind."

They both turned to the bar.

Jack got into it saying, "Listen, I did tell Norm don't worry about us getting raided."

Carl Webster looked around, his elbow on the bar.

"I thought I'd pay a fine," Jack said, "and we'd be back in business, the way I heard it works. You say we can defend ourselves, that's different. Let's get out the guns."

"We'll take care of it," Carl said. He turned to the bar and picked up his whiskey.

Jack waited. He wanted to yell at them to look at him, goddamn it. It was like when his mom and dad used to argue about what to do with him and he's standing there listening, looking from one to the other. His mom saying he was a spoiled brat, the same as Norm Dilworth did. What took Jack by surprise, Norm thinking he was fooling around with Heidi. He never believed Norm was wary or smart enough to notice anything going on. Then Norm saying there hadn't been an idea of his yet that worked, and was thinking of pulling out, taking his cut and leaving.

All right, this Nestor, pretending to be a government agent, he'd come on a raid or he wouldn't. He came, it would be all right to shoot him. Good. That didn't seem to be a problem. But

Norm Dilworth leaving, taking Heidi with him, was something Jack would have to get busy on.

Nestor, still at the church this morning but ready to go, had pictured his twelve cars of Avengers spread across the front of the roadhouse, facing it, but changed his plan.

These whiskey people were criminals and would be armed. It was too late now to sneak up on them. They start firing they'd shoot holes in the radiators and the cars would sit there after, useless till they were repaired.

The way to do it, come down the road from the highway and pull up one behind the other on the shoulder. There'd be the ditch to cross and then the parking lot, about 150 feet of hardpack to the roadhouse, open ground, shouldn't be more than a few cars parked there this morning. He'd use the bullhorn, give the whiskey people time to come out. They didn't, he'd send his Avengers to advance across the open yard in their robes, holding up their torches.

Nestor had watched these men fire their rifles and picked out the ones who'd shot and killed three of the striking coal miners: the Wycliff brothers, aggressive young punks, and a fella name of Ed Hagenlocker Jr. that everybody called Son, born of some tramp his daddy had been seeing at the time. Son liked to brag his old man was now married to a woman name of Sylvia who was the widowed mother of Pretty Boy Floyd's girlfriend, Louly Brown. "A cute girl," Son Hagenlocker said. "I can see why Pretty Boy'd want to get on top of her."

Nestor issued these three Springfield army rifles from his personal store and would keep these boys close to him, the Wycliff brothers and Son, all dead shots, on the road behind the cars. He'd send the thirty Avengers toward the roadhouse in three waves, spread out, walking toward the front entrance with their torches.

They'd likely get shot at and some would go down. Well, in any action you had to expect taking casualties. At the Somme in 1916, during the Great War, the British Expeditionary Force lost 58,000 men in one day. Second battle of the Marne, 12,000 American boys were killed during the assault. Hell, from July to November the British counted 310,000 casualties trying to take Passchendaele during the Ypres offensive, and the town wasn't even that important. It's what happened in war, men got killed.

Tony Antonelli was pretty sure there'd be shooting, mortal wounds suffered, and he'd get to call it "The

Bloody Bald Mountain War." He could open the story with:

"It began with an imposter named Nestor Lott, a cold-blooded killer who wore a .45 automatic on each hip, a man who had no regard for human life. Nestor Lott had been dismissed by the Department of Justice as a special agent, but chose to continue his mission, not simply to close speakeasies but to destroy—"

No, first he'd have to tell about Nestor being hired by the coal operators to break the strike. How he got the Klan to help him. How they shot and killed three Italian miners, wounded seven others—

Or save the strike stuff, put it in further down in the story and concentrate on the raid in the opening with Nestor Lott the key figure, responsible for the shoot-out that ensued.

He could even call it that, "Shoot-out at Bald Mountain."

That would be perfect, if the roadhouse was called the Bald Mountain something or other, club, resort. On the title page a photo of the roadhouse with the sign prominently displayed. Where, when the gun smoke cleared, saw—put in the number of men lying dead. Tony had been out there a couple of times and met Jack Belmont and the girls—one in particular, Elodie, catching his eye—but **damn** if he could remember if there was a sign in front.

Tony got there before Nestor and the Klansmen arrived. Earlier, he'd been told something was going on at the Pentacostal church on the edge of town, went out there and saw them getting ready and had a chance to speak to a Klansman named Ed Hagenlocker Jr., who told him what was going on and didn't mind Tony writing his name in the notebook. He had talked to Ed Jr. once in Krebs—where everybody called him Son—Son telling where he was from and about his dad being married to Louly Brown's mother. This time Son told him they'd either blow up the roadhouse or set their torches to it, burn the liquor place to the ground.

Right after this Tony drove out to Bald Mountain that was all dark trees and not bald anywhere that he could see, rising behind the roadhouse. He pulled up in front and said, "Nuts." There wasn't a sign on it that said Bald Mountain or any name at all. No cars here either, and he realized his Ford Coupé could be in the middle of the action, end up with bullet holes in it. Tony drove around back to see six cars parked in the yard in a row facing the back of the place, Tony assuming they belonged to Belmont and people who worked for him and didn't want their cars shot up. Tony left his car and walked around to the front. So far he hadn't seen a soul or any sign of life.

Not until he walked in the barroom, empty in dull morning light, and one of the bouncers appeared out of the back of the room and went behind the bar. Tony watched him reach underneath and come up with a revolver in each hand he laid on the bar. Now he set up a bottle of whiskey and a glass and poured a generous double shot. The bouncer's name was Walter. Not Wally, Walter. He saw Tony standing in the middle of the room and said, "We're closed."

It was in Tony's mind to say, **You better be,** but kept quiet. If they didn't know Nestor was coming and he said anything about it, he'd be intruding on the natural passage of events; he'd be putting himself in the story and have to explain why he tipped them off, these people selling liquor illegally. He didn't think **True Detective** would go for it.

Tony had asked Walter one time how he became a bouncer. Walter said he'd worked in oil fields and liked to get into fistfights. He was a big boy in his thirties, two hundred pounds or more on a Charles Atlas kind of build. Had a neck on him like a tree trunk and never smiled, nothing Walter thought was ever funny.

Now a man about fifty was coming down from upstairs putting on his suitcoat, his necktie hanging loose. Down the staircase Belmont must've picked up at an estate sale, once in the home of some guy who went out his office window in '29. Tony could check, find out where they got the stairway. Or write it assuming that could easily have been the situation, lot of it had been going on. Tony watched the guy go to the bar and pick up the whiskey waiting for him. He could be a lawyer or somebody in the oil business. Tony wondered if the man had been with Elodie. The times he was here before he'd seen her sitting in that plush area toward the back of the room, an arrangement of upholstered pieces, chairs and settees done in red damask to show off the whores. Elodie could be this man's favorite, spent the night with her while his wife thought he was in Tulsa. It got Tony wondering about Elodie, if she'd be all right when Nestor came on his raid—and my God, there she was.

Coming down the stairs in her pink kimono, her dark hair pinned up. The man at the bar raised his glass and she stepped over to give him a peck on the cheek. But now she was coming this way, the sweet girl, with a worried look on her face, Tony wishing more than anything in the world she wasn't a whore.

She offered her hands and he took them saying, "Where's everybody?"

"Busy," Elodie said. "You shouldn't be here."

He wanted to tell her, **You shouldn't either**. He

wanted to ask her to leave right now, run away with him and quit being a whore. But what he said was, "I saw them. Nestor and the Klan are on their way."

Jack Belmont was sitting on the side of the bed with Violet, his hand on her bare knee with her white shorts hiked up, his Winchester on the windowsill across the room, pointing out, a revolver on the floor over there.

Carl Webster appeared in the bedroom doorway.

"I don't see you're paying much attention."

"I'll hear their cars, won't I?"

"What if they leave 'em down the road?"

"I'm just getting a cigaret."

Violet put one between her lips, struck a kitchen match to light the cigaret and handed it to Jack. Violet had dark shiny hair and was maybe the best looking of the girls, Carl might say a beauty; he believed she had some Creek in her. Violet reminded him of a thin Narcissa Raincrow, his dad's housekeeper he slept with every night, only Violet was better looking. Carl now favored redheads with pure white skin and brown eyes; though he'd have to admit he liked Crystal Davidson's blonde hair, the way it was marcelled. Crystal was a few years older than Carl, while Louly Brown was a good five years younger but seemed grown up, the little girl with the cute smile who'd shot a wanted fugitive.

He said to Jack Belmont, "You don't fire less I tell you."

Carl walked a few strides along the upstairs hall to the next bedroom where Norm Dilworth was crouched at the front window with the Thompson, a 1921 model with a buttstock attached and a drum that held a hundred rounds of .45s. Norm had a pair of binoculars on the floor next to him. Heidi was stretched out on the bed, her head raised on pillows. She saw Carl and said, "Norm, Carl's here." That's all. She was quiet this morning, like Norm'd had a talk with her last night. Heidi had on a playsuit with bell-bottoms that looked Mexican to Carl. A .38 lay on the quilt next to her thigh.

Carl said to Norm, "You fire for range?"

"I lay it on the sill and get down behind it, these two nails holding it? It's set on the road."

"They could drive in."

"I raise up, keep the barrel on the sill."

It wasn't a minute later they heard a girl's voice yelling something, sounding like it was coming from the stairs.

The voice brought Heidi upright on the bed. "Lord, that's Elodie. Something's wrong."

Now they heard her in the hall and Carl stepped out of the bedroom to see Elodie coming toward him wide-eyed saying, **"Tony saw them—they're on their way."**

Carl stopped her, resting his hand on her shoulder. "Who's Tony?"

"The writer," Elodie said, sounding out of breath.

"I don't think I know him," Carl said. But there he was coming along the hall in a hurry, an eager young guy in a suit, a full head of combed hair. Carl said, "Who're you with, one of the newspapers?"

Now he looked surprised saying, "I write feature stories for **True Detective.**"

"No kidding," Carl said. "That's a good magazine."

"You read it?"

"When I get a chance."

They heard Norm in the room yell out, "Carl, they're here!" And yelled Carl's name again while Carl stood in the hall with Tony Antonelli.

He said, "You the one gonna interview Louly Brown in Tulsa, at the Mayo Hotel?"

Tony said, "How'd you know that?"

"I'll tell you right now," Carl said, "she isn't Charley Floyd's girlfriend or ever was. So don't ask her."

Tony followed the marshal into the bedroom, Carl Webster in person, here, to meet Nestor Lott and his Klansmen. Tony couldn't believe it. He'd try to stay close to him.

They could see the cars coming in from the highway, about a quarter of a mile to the road and turning into it, one behind the other coming past the woods that stood at the north end of the property. Now they were slowing to a stop, closing up almost bumper to bumper across the front of the yard, Norm saying, "The lead car's Nestor's, the De Soto. There he is getting out. See him?"

Carl said, "He's a little fella, huh?"

Tony said, "This is the first time you've seen him?"

Heidi, standing over Norm, was in the way. Carl Webster moved her aside and said, "Go tell Jack not to fire till I tell him. I want to see how Nestor wants to work it."

Heidi left in a hurry, not saying a word, and now Norm asked, "What's that he's holding?"

"A bullhorn," Carl said.

Tony got out his notebook and started writing, describing Nestor standing in the road behind his dark blue De Soto four-door sedan. Now two more with army rifles joining him. Now a third one, also with a Springfield coming out of the car and Tony said, "I know that one, he's called Son. He says his dad's married to the mother of Pretty Boy Floyd's girlfriend, Louly Brown?" Tony stopped as Carl turned to look at him, but then said, "I can't help what he says, can I?"

"He doesn't know what he's talking about," Carl said. "Write that in your notebook."

Tony wrote: "The marshal doesn't raise his voice but has an amazing presence (command?) and you want to believe what he says, even though he's still young. Wearing a navy blue two-piece suit, pressed. Maybe a sixth sense telling him this would be a memorable day. Impossible to tell where he carries his gun, a Colt .38 with a six-inch barrel. No hat this morning, the well-publicized panama he was wearing when he shot Emmett Long."

Carl picked up Norm's binoculars and studied the row of cars. "The ones sitting in there are wearing their robes, but not the three with Nestor. They're his shooters. Keep both your eyes on them. Nestor's wearing his old shield and a military decoration. It means this squirt was in the Great War, been in battle."

They heard a static sound from the bullhorn Nestor raised to his face.

Carl said, "Norm, put your sights on the last car." It's rear end was no more than ten feet from the edge of the woods. "That's where you'll start. Nestor's gonna give us five minutes to come out with our hands up or he'll . . . do whatever he feels like. As soon as he starts to talk rake those cars left to right across the tires, your finger stuck on the trigger. Get to his and stop. Let's see what they do."

Norm rested his front sight on the right rear tire of the last car.

Nestor said, "I'm giving you people five minutes—"

And Norm raked that line of coupés and sedans, the Thompson chattering from one end to the other, Carl watching through the glasses, Tony hunching his shoulders at the racket filling the room.

"You rose up on the two middle cars," Carl said. "I think you might've hit the ones inside."

"It got away from me," Norm said.

"Yeah, I can see blood on their robes. They're getting out the other side." Reporting it in a natural tone of voice while Tony made notes, seeing Klansmen piling out of the cars on the off-side to crouch behind them.

Now firing was coming from the next room, Jack Belmont snapping off shots. Carl lowered the glasses to look at Heidi.

"Go tell him I said to quit shooting."

Heidi ran to the other front bedroom to see Jack and Violet at the window, Jack firing at the cars. Heidi pushed Violet aside.

"The marshal says to quit shooting."

Jack said, "He did, huh?" levered the Winchester and fired another round before turning to look at Heidi.

She said, "He wants to see what they're gonna do next."

"They're armed," Jack said. "Ask him what he thinks they're gonna do."

Nestor was standing, looking over the De Soto's hood toward the roadhouse. Now he turned to the Klansmen hugging the ground behind their cars, all those white bedsheets that looked like piles of wash dumped in the road, a few pointed tops with eyeholes rising now to look through their car windows at the roadhouse. The Wycliff brothers and Son looked up at Nestor showing himself, hands on his hips, hat down on his eyes, looked at each other and got to their feet.

Nestor said to the Klansmen, "What's wrong with you? Come on, get up. They weren't trying to hit anybody, they're shooting at the tires."

A Klansmman said, "They's some here got shot."

"'Cause these people don't know how to fire a Thompson submachine gun. You got to hold her down," Nestor said. "I'm telling you they weren't trying to hit anybody, those boys got shot by accident. Come on, get out your torches and light 'em up. Cock your pistols and stick 'em in your pants, in front like I told you. I want to see you all advance on that position like nothing's gonna stop you. They see fire coming at 'em they'll panic, throw up their hands and run. I guarantee."

Norm said, "Carl? They're lighting torches. See 'em? Coming out from between the cars, across the ditch—"

"Lay it down in front of 'em," Carl said. "They'll stop and think about it." He watched them forming a line, ten across with their torches, holding them high. Carl thinking, Like the nitwit is saying, here, shoot me in the chest.

Norm, on his knees, raised the stock of the Thompson, getting the front sight on the middle of the yard.

Now another row of Klansmen was coming from between the cars with their torches, forming behind the first row.

Counting the ones still hiding back of the cars, Carl decided there were about thirty of them. He said to Norm, "Lay it down."

Norm fired left to right and with the clatter they watched the dirt kicked up about ten feet in front of the leading row, stopping them in their tracks, confused, pulling revolvers, turning into one another with their torches blazing, turning to Nestor behind his car.

Norm was grinning, watching them come near setting one another on fire. He said, "They don't know whether to piss or run home, do they?"

They aren't a hundred feet away," Jack Belmont said, "and he can't hit 'em? I should've kept the Thompson." He raised the Winchester and sighted against the black cross on a Klansman's chest, telling himself, Your first one. Take a breath and hold it, start to let it out . . .

"I think Carl just wants to stop them," Heidi said. "It looks like it did. They don't know what to do. Look at 'em." She was crouched next to Jack on the floor, holding the revolver he had given her.

Jack fired and saw the Klansman knocked off his feet, the torch flying.

"Got him."

He levered and fired.

"Got him."

Levered and fired.

"Another one. Shit, this is like fish in a barrel."

Levered and fired.

"How many's that?"

Levered and fired and handed the Winchester to

Heidi. "You counting? Keep track while you load that for me." He took the revolver she was holding and the one on the floor by his knee and fired one and then the other at arm's length, moving his head from gun to gun, fired at the cars and the bedsheets squeezing between them. "Now they're running across the road. Look, they're out in that pasture, some cows grazing there." Jack raised the revolvers and fired at them long range until he heard the guns click empty.

Heidi said, "Jack," touching his shoulder.

"Let me have the rifle."

"I didn't load it," Heidi said. "Carl's here."

Jack turned to Carl above him looking out the open window at the Klansmen lying in the yard, none of them moving. Tony, his notebook open, was standing next to him.

Carl said, "I told you to quit shooting."

Jack said, "You did? I must not've heard you. I know I got those seven out there, maybe a couple more. I fired at some I could see through the car windows, and they took off across the pasture over there. I fired a few shots at them."

"You hit a cow," Heidi said. "See the one like it's limping? Look, quick, now it's lying down. I think you killed it."

"I have to admit," Jack said, "firing at those bedsheets was like a shooting gallery, but I stopped them, didn't I? Heidi says she lost count." He looked up again at Carl Webster. "How many is it you've shot in your life? Just the four I've heard of?"

Carl, staring out the window, didn't answer him, Nestor on his mind.

Now Tony looked at the line of cars, steam rising out of a couple of their radiators, and made a note of it.

Carl said, "Where's Nestor?"

Jack looked out the window.

"Running, I imagine."

Carl said, "The ones in the pasture are all wearing robes."

"Then he's still behind the cars."

Tony got ready to speak as Carl said, "And the three boys with him? They didn't run. And if they're not lying out in the yard, where are they?"

It was quiet outside and in the room that smelled of gunpowder. Tony made a note of it and said, "I caught a glimpse of Nestor and those three—the ones with army rifles?—sneaking along behind the cars while Jack was shooting. They got to that last car and, I'm pretty sure they ducked into the trees."

Again it was quiet until Carl said, "So they're still around. Good."

8

They followed the marshal downstairs, Norm with the Thompson under his arm, Jack behind him, a revolver in each hand, Jack thinking how easy it would be to raise one of the .38s and shoot Norm in the back of the head, stick the barrel in that thatch of dark hair. Stumble against him as he fired and say oh my God, it was an accident. Jack felt good and said to Heidi over his shoulder, "I want it known I didn't shoot any cow."

She was carrying his Winchester and said, "I saw you, you did it on purpose."

"It must've stepped in a hole, why it fell down."

He felt like talking, proud of himself shooting those dumbbells coming with their torches. Wasn't anything to it. Lever and fire and watch them get knocked off their feet. He'd have to wait for the right time to get Norm, now wanting Norm looking at him when he did it. He wouldn't mind getting the drop on Nestor Lott and plug him, too.

Carl had the two bouncers with revolvers and pick handles at the front windows downstairs, on either side of the entrance, guys Norm had hired: Walter the fistfighter and the other one they called Boo, who'd been in a storage tank fire and was lucky to get out alive. From his left profile Boo could be taken for William Boyd, the movie star. He turned his head and Carl saw his right ear had been burnt off, the skin on his face red and shiny. One eye was gone and he wore smoked glasses day and night to hide his disfigurement.

Carl had the feeling he knew him. Not since he was in the fire, before that, up to a year ago. And had the feeling Boo was watching him, biding his time. He asked Norm what Boo's name was.

Norm said, "Billy Bragg. I hired him, he was selling whiskey his brother made, up in the Cookson Hills."

Carl was nodding. "I knew the brother, Peyton Bragg."

"You arrest him one time?"

"I shot him."

The two Negroes watched the back of the place from the kitchen, Franklin Madison and his grown son James, by an Indian woman. Carl had spoken to Franklin last night, learned the man had served on a frontier station out west and in Cuba in '98, the same war Virgil had fought in. Franklin had been married to a Chiricahua Apache woman, the daughter of a reservation jumper who'd been shipped to Oklahoma with Geronimo and that crowd. It gave them more things they had in common to talk about. Carl telling Franklin his grandmother was Northern Cheyenne, giving him some Indian blood. Franklin telling about the fight at Las Guásimas in Cuba where the Tenth saved Teddy Roosevelt's Rough Riders after he'd marched them into a jackpot. Carl had listened to him last night and got rifles for Franklin and James.

Outbuildings stood along the back of the property, what looked like a pump house, a tractor shed, a chicken house, then a thicket full of scrub standing behind the structures that became dense with redbud as the hill rose to Bald Mountain. Then, in the middle of the lot, the line of seven cars parked facing the house.

Carl said to Franklin, "You ever get a look at this Nestor Lott?"

Franklin said no, but he'd heard the man was evil, had those coal miners shot.

"He could sneak up behind the cars out there." They stood a good sixty feet from the back of the house. "I'll bet anything," Carl said, "Nestor won't want to go home till he's settled this."

"He's still here," Franklin said, "you won't have to track him."

Carl judged Franklin's age as close to seventy, a mostly bald black man with a sprinkle of white stubble over his jaw. They stood on either side of the kitchen window looking out at the yard, sunlight had given the cars a shine, but the sky closed in and now rain was coming down.

Franklin said, "What about the dead people in front? I know they ain't going nowhere, but was it all right to shoot 'em like that?"

"I have to phone Tulsa," Carl said, "ask my boss about it. I came here with another marshal, but I don't know where he is, or what he's doing."

Franklin said, "What if the sheriff come along?"

"Then the county'll look into it. The coroner will say those fools out there died of gunshot wounds, making it official. Then the county prosecutor will want to know who shot them, maybe have Jack Belmont brought up on manslaughter. That's if the Klansmen want to testify. But if they shouldn't be here in the first place, maybe they won't say anything. If the judge is in the Klan, that's something else."

"Will you appear?"

"If they charge Belmont."

"What if they don't?"

"Then I'll take him to Tulsa," Carl said, "and get him charged with **some**thing."

Carl glanced at the **True Detective** writer standing in the kitchen doorway. Tony waiting until Carl finished before saying, "You won't be able to make your call, they cut the telephone line. I tried it a minute ago."

Carl said, "So he's close by."

"You sound like it pleases you," Franklin said. He called out, "James?" And told his son to come in here.

Carl watched Franklin talking to him, James nodding, Franklin giving him an old converted Navy Colt from out of a kitchen drawer, winking at Carl. Now James took off his shirt. He walked through the bar to slip out the front in the cold rain.

"Gonna see if he can locate Nestor," Franklin said.

"He can do it," Carl said, "without getting shot?"

"James knows tricks from his mama's people," Franklin said. "How to stand almost in plain sight and you don't see him."

Nestor had picked Son to work around through the woods to where the telephone wire came out from the house. "Shimmy up the pole with a knife in your teeth, boy, and cut the wire, so they can't call anybody for help."

Son came back to the tractor shed with his arms skinned but had done the job.

Nestor looked out of the shed now to see the rain coming down hard to wash the cars parked back there and turn the yard dark. Man oh man, perfect. He could start making his move, not have to wait till night.

All three boys had been patient so far. Now they were acting restless and would voice their anger over the dead lying out front. Or they were putting it on, wanting to start shooting. Son telling him, "They's two of 'em show theirselves at that window," and raised his rifle to draw a bead. Nestor had to tell him to keep his pants on while he worked out what they'd do. How he'd set it up to take every last person in there.

One of the Wycliffs said, "Some of 'em's women."

"Whores," Nestor said.

Son was afraid somebody'd come along the road and see the bodies. Nestor said, "And keep driving, not wanting any parts of this business. Or going by they might only see the cars parked along the shoulder." But the boy was right, they had to get her done pretty soon. He said to the Wycliff brothers,

"You two think you could sneak out there, see if anybody left the key in their car?"

You bet they could, and slipped out of the shed to slither through the weeds, the cars between them and the back of the house. Watching them through a space between the boards, Nestor said, "You know their Christian names?"

All Son knew they was Wycliffs. Him and the brothers had never been close, other than when they were out burning crosses or throwing rocks at the Eyetalians, over in Sans Souci Park, the Eyetalians celebrating Mt. Carmel Day, whatever that was.

Nestor said, "Those boys must've fallen off the turnip truck, but they sure can shoot."

The Wycliffs came back to the tractor shed soaking wet and grinning at Nestor. Yeah, the Ford Coupé on the end and that black car right in the middle of the row both had keys in them. Nestor, pressed to the slit between the boards, said, "I believe it's a thirty-three Packard, the new one. Has that sporty look, a spare tire on each side. You know what they say, 'Ask the man who owns one.' I bet a dollar it's Jack Belmont's, but I ain't asking him nothing."

One of the Wycliffs said, "We gonna ride off in the Packard?"

Nestor said, "Hell no, we gonna bust in the house with it."

He had all three of the boys grinning at him now.

Jack Belmont wondered what they were waiting for, standing around in the semidark, Heidi next to him reloading his guns and placing them on the bar. The other girls were upstairs, the bartenders watching over them, and seeing what they could see from the windows.

"You want to tell me what we're doing?"

Speaking to Carl at the front entrance with the two bouncers, Carl holding one of the doors open, waiting for James to appear out of the mist. He said to Jack, "It's Nestor's call."

Jack held up his pocket watch trying to catch some light from the windows. "I can't even read my goddamn watch. He don't come pretty soon, I'm leaving. We aren't doing any business, those dead fools lying in the yard. I mean it, he don't start something, I quit. Come back when the sun's out."

Carl said, "You're going to Tulsa with me. You and that two-gun midget, if I can work it."

"You gonna arrest me? For what?" Like he couldn't believe it.

"There's seven people lying dead outside."

"Jesus Christ, what're you talking about— they're gonna burn down my place I didn't stop 'em. You saw 'em, with their goddamn torches?" Sounding a bit frantic and had to calm himself down. Trying to think of a way to do Norm—counting on Nestor starting a gunfight to give him the chance—and now the goddamn marshal wanted to arrest him. Saying if he could work it. **Telling** him that. He glanced at Norm sitting on the stairs with his Winchester now across his knees. Then turned to Carl at the front door.

Carl pushing it open and Jack saw the colored boy, James, come in with his old-fashioned Colt pistol, hair lying flat on his head, his body glistening wet. Jack watched James give Carl a nod and now the two of them were walking past him, going to the kitchen.

Jack followed behind saying, "You hear what I said? They're coming after **me**, with no right to do it's why I shot 'em. You know that."

The marshal didn't comment on it.

In the kitchen James laid his pistol on the counter by the window where Franklin handed him a dish towel. James dried his face before looking up at Carl. "I see these two come in the thicket from the lot, like they been up to the house."

Franklin was shaking his head. "I'd of seen 'em."

"Now the other two come out of the shed," James said, "and they all behind it, the little fella with the pistolas on him asking the two questions. I can't hear what they saying, but the little fella, he seem pleased by what they told him."

Franklin said it again, "They came up to the house I'd of seen 'em."

"Or they were looking at the cars," Carl said, "see who might've left a key."

Jack got on that saying, "Nobody works here leaves a key in their car. You can't trust our patrons. They leave here drunk, with drunk intentions. The only one might've been the **True Detective** writer." Jack looked around. "Where is he?"

"He's upstairs," Norm said. "I 'magine talking to Elodie. He was asking me about her—can't believe that nice-looking girl's a whore. I said give her three bucks and see what she does for you." Norm stood in the doorway to the main room, turning his head to look at Heidi now, in there at the bar. Norm said to her, "How much he give you for loading his gun?" Now he turned and was looking at Jack Belmont in the kitchen.

Norm giving him a hard stare.

It told Jack his old buddy'd had enough of his fooling with Heidi and meant to do something about it. For a few seconds Jack thought of staring back at him, get it out in the open between them, but caught himself in time. Where was the advantage in doing that? No, Jack grinned like he'd thought of something and turned to Franklin at the window.

"Franklin? You hear the one, the woman of the house asks her colored girl Dinah if her husband is a good provider? Dinah says, 'Yessum, he's a good providah, all right, but I'se always scared dat niggah's gwine get caught at it.'"

Jack was still grinning, waiting for Franklin to laugh.

Franklin nodded, looking like he was trying to smile. But now his gaze moved to the window again, Franklin saying, "They at the cars," his voice raised. "Sneaked up, getting in the one in the middle, the Packard. Backing out, behind the other cars now."

Carl, with him at the window, picked up the navy Colt from the counter, telling Franklin to fire through the windows of the cars in front, and they both began firing, not knowing if they were hitting the Packard or the ones in it. They paused and could hear the car's engine being throttled up, running high, and now they saw the black shape in the clear, streaking through the mist toward the trees on the far side of the lot and the drive that curved in from the road. But now it was slowing, starting to make a wide turn through the lot, churning up mud as the black Packard swung around to head toward the front of the roadhouse.

Son, at the wheel, began to brake coming on to the bodies lying in the empty parking lot. It turned Nestor from the windshield as the car came to a stop.

"What're you doing?" The man excited and showing it. "Roll over 'em, for Christ sake. They aren't gonna be any deader."

Son couldn't do it. He looked at the rearview mirror and told the Wycliff brothers to get out and pull the bodies out of the way, Nestor yelling at him, "Goddamn it, go on. You aren't gonna hit 'em all." Son shook his head. This time he turned to the Wycliffs in the backseat and told them to hurry up and get to it, drag 'em out of the way. The brothers felt the same as Son about running over the bodies. They hopped out of the car and started pulling them by the arms back toward the cars standing on the road.

Nestor, watching through the windshield, quieter now, said, "You're giving 'em time to get ready for us."

Carl told Jack and the bouncers, Walter and Boo, to get down behind the bar and wait till he saw what was going to happen. He expected an argument from Jack he wouldn't have time for, and when Jack asked him where he'd be, Carl didn't answer. He told Norm and Heidi to run upstairs and get the bartenders and wait up there in the hall.

"Don't show yourselves or come out to the stairs till somebody starts shooting."

Jack said to him again, "Where you gonna be?"

Carl said, "I want a word with this Nestor."

Son saw a clear fifty feet ahead of him now, plenty of room to make his turn and head directly for that big wooden front. The Wycliffs would come running behind the Packard with their rifles. Son gunned the motor, pressed down hard on the gas pedal and swerved toward the doors, Nestor yelling at him to "Bust through, bust 'em down!" and Son drove that Packard through the entrance, banging the doors off their hinges, pieces of lumber bouncing off the hood, smashing the windshield, a fragment coming past him like a spear, but they were inside, Nestor hanging on, his jaw clenched, and Son braked and plowed into tables and chairs that put Nestor up against the dashboard, the Packard plowing furniture to wedge it against a post in the middle of the room. Son turned his head to see a man in a suit and panama hat watching him from behind the bar, the guy standing there like he was the only one in the place.

Upstairs, Tony Antonelli heard the car smash through the front doors, heard the howl of the engine and knew what was happening down below. He had to stick his shirttail back in his pants and pull up his suspenders looking at Elodie on the bed in only a pair of lace panties, God Almighty, her ninnies pointing straight at him, her expression scared to death. He said, "Stay here, I'll come back to get you," and ran out of the room and down the hall past the bartenders reaching out too late to stop him. He had to pull his arm away from Heidi grabbing on to him and saw Norm waving at him from the other side of the hall to get back.

But Tony was at the top of the stairway now looking down at the Packard and the smashed furniture, and realized, damn it, he'd left his notepad in the bedroom.

He saw Carl Webster behind the bar facing Son getting out from behind the wheel, with a rifle, and now the Wycliff brothers were coming up on the driver's side of the car, both holding rifles he believed were Springfields. Tony judging the distance between the three locals and Carl Webster less than thirty feet.

He saw Nestor Lott come out of the front passenger side and move up to face Carl from across the car's hood. This was the tableau Tony committed to his memory, looking down not quite directly at the front of the Packard, but more to Nestor's side of the car. From this angle he could see Nestor holding a .45 automatic in each hand, below the level of the hood, close to the spare tire mounted there.

Carl, behind the bar, arms hanging at his sides—Tony thinking of the way he would write it—with a relaxed demeanor, would not see that Nestor was ready to shoot. Tony thinking he should yell out, but not wanting to involve himself, hesitating . . .

And Carl Webster got his attention.

Carl saying, "Am I speaking to Nestor Lott?"

"'Course you are," Nestor said. "Don't confuse me with these sharecroppers holding rifles on you. Where's everybody? I want to know who killed my boys. And where you stole that Thompson."

"I'm Deputy United States Marshal Carl Webster," Carl said. "I'm placing you under arrest for impersonating a federal officer. Wearing that badge like you deserve it."

"You see what else I got on my chest?"

"That medal," Carl said, "don't mean a thing to me."

"You ought to be ashamed of yourself," Nestor said. "Boy, you're on the wrong side of this shenanigan, working for the whiskey people. You ought to be over here with me."

"I've told you," Carl said, "you're under arrest. My partner has the warrant."

Tony watched Carl turn his head to the three locals with their army rifles. Carl said to them, "You people can go or stay. You stay, I'll arrest you for helping this monkey break the law. Which is it gonna be?"

Son and the Wycliff brothers didn't stir, their rifles pointing at the bar, Tony would bet, waiting for Nestor to give the word. He heard Carl tell them, "Put down your guns."

The locals still didn't move, covering the marshal with their Springfields. Tony would remember the marshal standing with his arms at his sides, **his demeanor relaxed as he looked at sudden death staring him in the face.** Now Nestor was saying, "Call your people out. They upstairs? I want to see what we have here." Tony would write: **No one moved. All waiting for Nestor's deadly signal, firing the first shot.**

But now Carl said to Nestor, "Let me see your hands. Lay 'em on the hood there."

For a few moments the room was quiet, Tony looking down at the four men by the car, Carl facing them, Tony pretty sure Carl knew about Nestor and his two guns and that Nestor's game was to bring on a gunfight, but only on his terms. Now Nestor was speaking.

"Marshal, you have it ass-backwards. It's your hands I want to see. Bring out your gun and lay it there on the bar."

Tony turned his gaze on Carl Webster.

Carl saying, "I want to be clear about this so you understand. If I have to pull my weapon I'll shoot to kill."

Amazing—the same words, according to Crystal Davidson, Carl had said to Emmett Long before he shot him. Tony sure of it—he could hear Crystal telling it again in that suite at the Georgian hotel in Henryetta, Tony and the roomful of newsmen writing it down. **If I have to pull my weapon** . . .

"Show me you understand," Carl said to Nestor, "by laying your hands on the hood."

Tony, above the scene, saw it about to happen.

Nestor thumbing back the hammers on his .45s, one and then the other, starting to bring them up, Tony staring at the .45s clearing the Packard's hood . . .

And saw Carl extending his Colt .38 straight out over the bar—had it already drawn in that split second of time—and shot Nestor, **bam,** filling the room with that hard sound, and shot Son, **bam,** and saw Jack Belmont behind the bar now, and the bouncers Walter and Boo bringing up their revolvers, and it stopped the Wycliff brothers, surprised the hell out of them—heads popping up from behind the bar—and **bam,** Carl shot the first one as more gunfire filled the room, coming from either side of Tony at the top of the stairs, but he made himself keep looking at the scene, at Jack Belmont holding a Winchester and looking up this way like he was checking on Heidi, concerned about her as the second Wycliff fired the rifle wedged against his side and Tony saw bottles on the shelf behind Carl shatter and mess up the mirror, saw Carl extend his Colt and shoot him, **bam,** as this second Wycliff was throwing the bolt of his rifle to put a round in the breech. Now the one-eyed bouncer was firing, shooting the Wycliff boy again before he went down. Tony saw Carl turn to Nestor, even though he was already dead, Tony knowing it because Carl knew it, or he'd have shot him again. It got Tony thinking of Carl's words, **If I have to pull my weapon I'll shoot to kill.**

But how'd he pull it so fast? How did he get it out from under his coat in that split second? Carl was reloading his gun, taking bullets from the side pocket of his coat. He walked around the end of the bar and went over to the other side of the Packard to take a look at Nestor.

Tony came down to stand next to him to see Nestor dead and tell Carl Webster something.

"When he asked you to bring out your gun"— Tony hesitated saying it—"you told him the same thing you told Emmett Long. Word for word."

Carl said, "I did?"

"Crystal Davidson told us, that time at the hotel."

"You remembered it?"

"I wrote it down. Everybody in the room did. Now you said the same thing and proved it, shooting three more."

"Four," Carl said.

Tony paused before saying, "You're right."

"Any of 'em shot by these bozos," Carl said, "were already dead."

Tony looked up at the tin ceiling. "My ears are still ringing." He looked down to see Carl give Nestor's gut a nudge with the toe of his shined black boot.

Carl turned to the stairs then as Heidi called out, "Jack? . . . Where's Jack?" and told them, "Norm's been shot. I think he's dead."

9

The first thing Bob McMahon told Carl, seated across the desk, he was getting time off while they investigated the roadhouse shootings. Carl would make his statement and they'd see how it compared to what witnesses said, all the ones on the scene. Carl said, "You aren't taking my word?"

"Your account," McMahon said, "you shot all four once they were in the place, Nestor Lott and the three boys with him."

Carl nodded saying, "I was trying out a new Colt thirty-eight special on a forty-five-caliber frame."

"That's a heavy weapon."

"Less kick to it. You hit where you point it."

"The bouncers"—McMahon looked at pages of reports on his desk—"Walter and that one-eyed guy, Boo Bragg, they claim they shot two of them."

"They want the credit," Carl said, "they can have it, but Nestor and his boys were already dead or dying. Talk to the **True Detective** writer. He saw the whole show."

"He was here this morning," McMahon said, "Anthony Antonelli. He said you told Nestor Lott if you pulled your weapon you'd shoot to kill. You remember saying that to him?"

"If I had to pull it," Carl said.

"You remember saying it to Emmett Long? That time it was his girlfriend told us, Crystal Davidson?"

"After I told him he was under arrest. It was the same thing here, they could put their weapons down, but if they intended to use them I'd have to shoot."

"Anthony says he's never seen a gun appear so fast."

"You ask him how many gunfights he's seen?"

"What he's saying, he didn't see you draw. He looked over, your gun's out and you're firing."

"What part of that bothers him?"

"He wants to know if you were holding it in your hand," McMahon said, "below the counter."

"I gave 'em a chance to put down their guns," Carl said, staring back at his boss. "They didn't do it."

"Were you holding your weapon or not?"

"I was holding it."

"The Tulsa paper said you drew and fired."

"They asked me if I shot all four," Carl said. "I told 'em yes, I did. They didn't ask if my gun was already in my hand."

"They like the idea of a marshal with a quick

draw," McMahon said, and looked down at his papers. "Anthony wants Belmont arrested for stealing his car."

"I know. I told him he shouldn't of left the key in it. I was sure the Packard was Jack's but he never said it was."

McMahon was staring at him again. "I notice you always refer to Belmont by his first name. Like you know each other pretty well."

"I know him," Carl said. "Set me loose I'll find him for you."

"Where you think he is?"

"The first place I'd look is Kansas City."

McMahon said after a few moments, "Maybe."

"He'd fit right in."

"You know for a fact he killed those Klansmen?"

"As fast as he could. Norm Dilworth shot the two in their car. The Thompson got away from him."

"And you believe Belmont shot and killed Dilworth."

"I know he did, so he could have Norm's wife," Carl said. "Check the round they took out of Norm. Was it from a Winchester or a Springfield oh-three?"

"It went through him and through the house," McMahon said. "It's outside in that thicket. And I doubt anyone who was there, the bouncers, the bartenders, will admit seeing Belmont shoot him."

"They don't work for him now," Carl said.

"But they don't have a reason to name him. Even if we find those guys, I don't see they'll do us any good. And this Heidi Winston, you think she ran off with him?"

"I guess so. Unless he twisted her arm."

"I doubt she minds him being the son of oil money."

They were both quiet for several moments.

Carl said, "You remember Peyton Bragg, a couple years ago? Cooked whiskey and robbed banks? That half-ugly, one-eyed bouncer's his kid brother."

"Does he know who you are?"

"I believe so, but he hasn't said anything."

"We have a warrant out on him?"

Carl said, "The Volstead. We can get about anybody on that one."

They were quiet again, both of them with their thoughts for about a minute this time.

McMahon said, "I don't see how you let Belmont get away."

"I made a mistake," Carl said. "He's acting like he had a good time shooting those people, nothing to it. I told him I was taking him in."

"For irritating you?"

"I wasn't sure if there'd be a charge against him."

"For shooting people coming to burn his house down?"

"Yeah."

"So you wanted to hand him over to a prosecutor," McMahon said, "but you let him slip away. At the time Dilworth was shot, what were you doing?"

"Nobody knew about it till Heidi called out he'd been hit."

He paused and McMahon said, "Yeah . . . ?"

"She said she thought he was dead."

McMahon waited.

"I'd gone around to the other side of the Packard to look at Nestor lying there. I saw the medal for bravery he'd pinned on his chest, a Distinguished Service Cross from the war. My dad won a medal for bravery in Cuba."

McMahon saw him frowning now.

"But Nestor—Jesus—wasn't anything like my dad."

They sat on the porch of that big California bungalow among pecan trees in the evening, having their drinks before supper, Virgil with the pile of newspapers the Texas oil people brought whenever Carl Webster's name appeared, this time with pictures.

"You sure like that hat. You're turning into a regular jelly bean, aren't you?"

They were drinking sour mash over ice with a slice of orange and a little sugar, Virgil's favorite. "'Twelve Slain at Roadhouse,'" Virgil said, reading a headline. You shoot four of 'em and they give you a vacation, huh? That's a pretty good deal."

Carl let his dad talk.

"The newspapers are eating this one up. Can't get enough. Some more reporters come by yesterday, and that one with **True Detective,** Anthony Antonelli? He says he's writing a story about it. Gonna call it 'Gunfight at Bald Mountain.'"

"I didn't know he was coming right away."

"Wants to do what he called cover stories about you and another one on Jack Belmont. Wants to ask you about all the bad guys you had to shoot. How many is it now, eight counting the cow thief? He says he's gonna ask you if you told each one the same thing, if you pulled your weapon you'd shoot to kill."

"I'm stuck with that," Carl said.

"It's what happens you become a famous showoff. You have to keep track of what you said. You get a name for shooting outlaws, one'll come along, try and shoot you to make his own name. Something this Jack Belmont could have in mind. Anthony says he wants to ask Jack why he robs banks and sells bootleg liquor when his dad's richer'n sin. I told him the boy either wants to embarrass his daddy or show him up. How many people has Jack shot, the seven at the roadhouse?"

"One before that, when he was fifteen."

"Same as you."

They let it hang.

"His dad's Oris Belmont," Carl said.

"I know who he is. But what can he offer his boy? Work up there in the office with him? Get to look out the window at Tulsa? Or he can clean out storage tanks if he wants. I said to Anthony, take me and Carl, we have the same situation here. I'm fairly rich and Carl don't make much more'n a few thousand a year, but we don't compete with each other."

"No, I listen to you tell me your opinion of things," Carl said.

"I advise you. I give you the opportunity to become a famous pe-can planter, eek out a living hitting trees with a fishing pole. I tell you, stay out of the oil business. Right now it's down around four bits a barrel 'cause there's too much of it. That East Texas field come in and I'm making less than four cents a barrel." He reminded Carl the governor of Oklahoma, Alfalfa Bill Murray, had put every producing well in the state under martial law, armed guards on over three thousand wells until the price went up to a dollar a barrel. "It could take a while, but it'll come back. You know why?

There's so many people own cars now, and there more every day."

Carl said, "You're not broke?"

"Honey, I been making royalties since the Glenn Pool come in," Virgil said. "Like I told Anthony, I'm fairly rich. What I didn't tell him, I keep out a good hundred thousand in cash at all times—"

"Where?"

"In the house. It's enough to live like a third-rate king for a good twenty years. The rest, I got a few filling stations and cafés with a business partner. People have to buy gas to run their cars and they have to eat."

"You keep a hundred thousand dollars in the house?"

"And a few guns. Don't worry about it," Virgil said. He sipped his whiskey and said, "You're not here, the reporters start asking me questions. They follow me out to the orchard wanting to know what I do with all my money. See, they'd noticed the wells pumping. First they ask me what I think about my only son on the trail of fugitive outlaws and bank robbers. I said, after the crash of '29 I didn't think there was any money left in the banks to rob. They want to know if I went bust. I told them we ever get Repeal I'm opening a few saloons somewhere. Not here, we're dry as a bone on account of we was Indian Territory not too long ago. That and the Baptists, this state'll vote dry forever. I told them hell no I ain't broke, I got investments. They said you can still go broke. I said not how I'm set up, I'd still live the life of a second-rate king. I thought about it since, five thousand a year for twenty years, and changed it to a third-rate king."

"You told them," Carl said, "you had cash put away?"

"Never did, but that's what they kept asking, if I'd hide away money. I told 'em it was none of their business. They're the nosiest people I ever met."

Carl said, "What'd you say to make 'em think you'd put away cash? If you're gonna live like a second-rate king—"

"Third-rate."

"It means you have money to do it with."

"I never said a word about my money."

"You told them you had guns in the house and you were a crack shot?"

"They're asking me later on about being with Huntington's Marines in the Spanish War. That's all."

"You tell them you won a medal for bravery?"

"For getting shot by a sniper." Virgil took a good sip of his drink and said, "This writer, Anthony Antonelli? Said you told him you'd be home."

"I was in Henryetta yesterday."

"You still crave that gun moll?"

"Some oil man's been seeing her, thinks he's daring. Crystal and I had supper, talked about different things. I like her, but it don't mean I want to marry her. You know she lived with Emmett Long after he killed her husband. It's the same with Heidi Winston, the girl that ran off with Jack Belmont."

"You can talk to those people?"

"I can ask questions. What's it like being with a man's wanted dead or alive? I ask Crystal if she was scared all the time. She says, 'Well, sure.' But she sounded surprised, like it was something she hadn't thought about. Being scared was so natural to her. Heidi's different, she was a whore and I think she likes the excitement for a change. At the roadhouse she's kidding Jack about shooting a cow, saying he did it on purpose. Right below them out the window are seven dead guys he shot lying in the yard."

Virgil said, "There's no way to understand people like that."

Carl told him Nestor Lott had a Distinguished Service Cross pinned to his coat he must've won during the war.

"When you shot him?"

"I almost hit the medal."

"I imagine you were more dead center," Virgil

said. "It sounds like he wanted everybody to know he'd been a hero at one time. If it was his medal."

"I'm pretty sure it was. The man had no feelings," Carl said, "but when the time came to stand up, he did."

Virgil said, "You run into some strange birds, don't you?"

Narcissa Raincrow appeared from the kitchen holding her drink, whiskey and Coca-Cola, to tell them supper was ready.

They sat at the round table in a back corner of the kitchen, windows on two sides, pecan trees everywhere you looked out there.

Narcissa served them steak and eggs and potatoes, all of it fried, a bowl of leftover white beans with salt pork, a loaf of bread she'd baked and a dish that looked like sauerkraut with tomato sauce on it. Narcissa sat down at the table and listened to them talk about Franklin Roosevelt winning the presidential election, happy that he'd skunked that constipated Herbert Hoover.

"Will Rogers says the Democrats have gone in," Virgil told them, "with all kinds of promises to regulate the stock exchange, help out the farmers, support veterans' pensions, and they'll come out with all kinds of alibis. Will Rogers says we don't vote for a candidate, we vote against the other one."

"Says he never met a man he didn't like," Carl said. "You believe that?"

"No, I don't," Virgil said, "but it sounds good. You know when he was in vaudeville doing rope tricks and talking, he'd twirl two ropes at the same time, the idea to set one loop on the horse and the other one over the rider. Will Rogers had a list of things he'd made up to say if he missed. Like, 'If I don't loop one on soon, I'll have to give out rain checks.' Or he'd say, 'This is easier to do on a blind horse, he don't see the rope coming.' He'd get so many laughs making excuses he'd muff a rope trick on purpose so he could say something funny about it."

Carl said, "You're sure full of Will Rogers lore, aren't you?"

"He's a movie star, he appears on the stage, he writes a newspaper column full of misspelled words—he's our greatest American, the funniest man I ever heard speak."

"And he's part Indian," Narcissa said.

"He's nine-thirty-fourths Cherokee," Virgil said, "a quarter Indian if you fudge it. Will Rogers'd say, 'We didn't come over on the **Mayflower,** we met it.'" Hunched over his supper plate Virgil said to Carl, "You remind me of him sometimes. I don't know why but you do."

Carl said, "I can think of all kinds of people I don't like, so that ain't it."

"You're both kind to animals," Virgil said. "You're modest in your way, or know how to put it on. Remember seeing him in the Ziegfeld Follies that time? You were just a kid then."

Only a few days after Carl had shot the cow thief out of his saddle. He nodded to his dad, remembering chorus girls with long white legs tap-dancing around the stage and Will Rogers coming out in black chaps and a hundred feet of rope coiled in his hand, his range hat cocked to one side, hair hanging on his forehead. Carl remembered the cow thief's name was Wally Tarwater.

Virgil was saying, "She keeps shoving this sauerkraut at me claiming it's good for you."

"It is," Narcissa said. "Ellen Rose Dickey in her radio talk says it's the perfect health food. I sent away to Clyde, Ohio, for fifty recipes. I put ground-up pecans in it. I put onions in it and made a tomato sauce to put on it. He pushes it away."

"It smells," Virgil said.

"You smell and you don't know it," Narcissa said, "'cause you have B.O. I buy Lifebuoy soap at the store. He don't wash under his arms with it every day like I tell him. No, once a week he takes his bath. I tell him to wash his mouth with Listerine. He don't have time reading his papers. I tell him Listerine kills two hundred million germs in only fifteen seconds. He still don't have time. I try to get him to eat Fleischmann's yeast every day, three cakes, so he can be regular sitting on the toilet. I hear him groaning in there trying to make poo-poo. No, he says he don't need Fleischmann's yeast. You see how he's losing his hair? I try to get him to use this tonic they call Hair-Medic. He won't do it. I tell him the famous Harry Richman likes to use it. I tell him Ruth Etting the singer uses it. She says it does wonders for her scalp. Virgil says he don't need it. Virgil reads about Ideal Manhood in my **Physical Culture** magazine, that old guy Bernarr Macfadden showing you how to exercise? Virgil don't get out of his chair. I send for the free book of Charles Atlas, how Dynamic Tension gives you everlasting health and strength. He won't read it. I get him Earle Liederman's book that tells how to strengthen your inner organs. I send to Newark, New Jersey—maybe he'll like Lionel Strongfort's book, how to energize your body. Virgil don't even open it. He says, 'Strongfort, you kidding me? The guy made up that name.'"

Virgil said, "Tell him how you bought a tube of Ipana on account of my pink toothbrush."

Narcissa was shaking her head, worn out, through with him.

"I use Ipana now," Virgil said. "I get a new toothbrush and she stays white." He chewed on a piece of steak he'd dipped in his egg yolk and said to Carl, "Did you know thirty thousand people a year are killed in car wrecks? They must be out on the road trying to run into each other." He said, "I just read that," and looked at Narcissa. "What was it in, **Liberty?**"

"I believe **Liberty,**" she said. "Or it was in **Psychology,** the one that's called **Life in the Modern World?**"

10

The first time Crystal saw Carl's apartment she had come to Tulsa on a shopping trip. He showed her around the two-bedroom place, where he'd been living since joining the marshals, saying he paid thirty a month for it furnished, including heat and light, a new kitchen, the sleeping porch in back . . . Crystal said, "Not bad." He told her he was due to repaint the walls and lay new carpeting, but hadn't done anything but hang those pictures in the living room. He waited for Crystal to wander over to the wall of framed photographs, some of them enlarged.

"That's my dad in uniform, when he was a seagoing marine." He waited until she was close enough to touch the photo before saying, "He was on the **Maine.**"

By this time he'd said the same thing to all the different girls who'd been here during the past few years: "He was on the **Maine.**" And every one of them knew what happened in Havana Harbor in 1898 and listened to him describe how Virgil was blown off the ship when it exploded and into a Spanish prison.

"You told me about your dad," Crystal said. "One of those afternoons you stopped by."

"When you were still in the farmhouse?"

"It wasn't long after you shot Emmett. You told me about all these people, your family, your life when you were a little kid." She turned enough to look at him. "I had the feeling you wanted me to see you as a regular guy, not a dumb cop or some-one, all you do is shoot people." Crystal turned to the wall of photos again saying, "I've never seen these, but I bet I can pick out your people from what you told me about them." Crystal nodded to a photo. "This is your mother. I believe her name is Grace?"

"Graciaplena," Carl said, "Full of Grace. But that's my grandmother, not my mother. She's part Northern Cheyenne."

"My mistake," Crystal said. "If she's part Indian then you are, too." She looked at him again with a faint smile. "I would never of suspected."

"The first time I met Emmett, at the drugstore, he said it made me a breed. That's me in the cow-boy outfit when I was four. My dad bought it for me. He wanted to be a cowboy when he was a kid. Fifteen years old he bought a horse for five dollars, thought he'd ride off and find work on a spread.

But his stepdad, a preacher with the Church of the Most Holy Word, sold the horse from under him and kept the money. He joined the marines instead, still only fifteen, and his mom ran off to Lame Deer, Montana, to live with her people. She's still there, but I've never met her. Or my mother, she died having me. That's Grace in the white dress the day they got married in Havana. That's her dad with her, Carlos, the one I was named for. I met him one time my dad took me to Cuba. Those are some of my dad's oil wells. There's the two of us on a derrick platform when I was a kid. He likes to pose."

"That's where you get it," Crystal said.

"But he's no oil man. Even with the checks coming in he keeps working his pecan trees."

"He must've spoiled you when you were a kid."

"Virgil always bought me good horses. I worked stock from the time I was about twelve and could ride like a man, right up till I joined the marshals. That enlarged shot of the house? That's my dad and Narcissa and me on the front porch the day we moved in. We used to live down on the county road, where you turn into the property. Narcissa's his housekeeper."

Crystal said, "I bet she's more than that."

"Yeah, well, they're close, been together twenty-six years now. Narcissa takes good care of him. He reads newspapers and she reads magazines and they tell each other things. I drive down to

Okmulgee weekends I get the chance. My dad and I sit on the porch and talk."

"Couple of pards, huh?"

"He likes to hear what I'm up to."

"When you could be living on the homestead?"

"Yeah, picking nuts. But he's always let me have my head."

"He must wonder though."

"What I like about being a marshal? He thinks I'm a show-off, out to make a name for myself."

She said, "You are, aren't you?"

Carl grinned at her and Crystal came over to take him by the arm toward his bedroom, Crystal saying, "Can we make it a quickie so I can get out of here, please, and go shopping? How about if I just pull up my skirt and take my panties off?"

"You're wearing panties?"

"Honey, I told you, I'm going to Vandever's, see what's new. And try not to muss up my hair for a change, okay?"

This morning he got home from his dad's place and took a shower standing in the tub, shaved and combed his hair, wetting the comb to get a straight part and rubbed bay rum on his face. He'd wear the vest that was part of his dark suit. It was cold out, too cold for the panama. He'd wear his brown felt, get used to it over the next couple of winter months, the hat taking on a good shape and he liked the feel of it, pinching the front of the crown to drop it on his head and knowing it looked good, a slight curve to the brim. He didn't care for overcoats. When he was in the country he'd wear a cowboy coat, a fleece-lined over his suit. In towns, in and out of cars, a raincoat was enough. He picked out a burgundy necktie to go with his blue shirt and the dark blue suit and slipped on his shoulder holster. Wearing his revolver on his hip was a little more comfortable, but the big Colt on the .45 frame was easier to pull from under his left arm and he could pull it sitting down. He spun the cylinder to check the loads and slipped the revolver, its front sight filed down, into the holster he softened every couple of weeks with saddle soap. He put a fresh pack of Luckies in his coat pocket and a book of matches, but left the Beechnut scrap on the bureau—what he chewed sometimes when he was in the country or at his dad's place; his dad loved that Beechnut scrap. He slipped a pair of handcuffs into a pocket of the raincoat—he didn't like the hard metal feel of the cuffs on the back of his belt. Spare rounds were always in his suitcoat pocket. What else? His wallet, change, a pack of gum, the keys to the Pontiac Eight sedan they were letting him use. Nine minutes later he pulled up in front of the Mayo Hotel. In the lobby he glanced at himself in a mirror, lifted his hat and eased it down a bit closer on his eyes, the brown hat working, Deputy Marshal Carl Webster looking good.

11

Carl knocked on the door of 815. It opened and Tony Antonelli was standing there looking at him. Carl said, "I understand you want to talk to me."

"Yeah, but not now. I'm about to interview Louly Brown."

"You haven't started yet?" Carl said. "Lemme just say hi to her." He could tell the **True Detective** writer didn't want him to come in, but had to step aside as Carl moved past him to look around at a sitting room. Now Tony motioned to a door.

"She's in the bedroom."

"You got her a whole suite of rooms?"

"Two rooms and bath, fifteen dollars."

"There's good money in writing, huh?"

"It's on an expense account." Tony raised his hand and said, "Wait a minute, I'll check on her." He walked to the bedroom door, rapped with one knuckle twice and said, "Louly?"

Carl could hear her voice but not the words, Tony saying, "Yeah?" Saying, "That's a shame." And finally, "Of course I'll wait." He turned to Carl. "She says she's got a darn pimple and is trying to hide it."

"What is she," Carl said, "a movie star? Tell her I'm here waiting to see her."

"She's quite self-conscious," Tony said, "bashful, all this attention more than she can handle."

Carl turned around and sat down in a big, comfortable chair at the end of the sofa. He looked up to see Tony coming over, Tony saying, "If we have a few minutes, I'd like to hear about the shootings you were in, ones I only read about in the paper. I had to dig back in the clip morgue at the Tulsa **World** to get the one called 'Gunfight at Close Quarters' and the other one, 'Marshal Shoots Machine-Gun Killer from Four Hundred Yards.'"

Carl said, "Those were the only two. The one was like most situations like that and the other wasn't a gunfight."

"I was in Kansas City on and off last year trying to get the lowdown on Boss Pendergast and his cronies. Good luck to any journalist who wants to try." Tony went on talking as he sat down at the end of the sofa, on the edge of the cushion and got out his notebook. "I'd like to hear about the one where you used a rifle."

"You mention Kansas City," Carl said, "I'm thinking of going there."

Tony said, "Well . . . it's the biggest city in area in the entire U.S., known as the Paris of the Plains. And it's wide open. K.C. has all the betting, booze, and babes anyone could want. I mean people who go in for that kind of stuff."

Carl said, "Have you seen Elodie?"

It straightened Tony. "Not since the other day."

"She's over at the courthouse talking to marshals. I told her, 'You go back to Seminole I'll put you in jail.'"

"I haven't seen her," Tony said. "She's at the courthouse, uh?"

Carl said, "You want to talk about Elodie or hear about a shoot-out?" See how professional this **True Detective** writer was.

It took him only two seconds to get back on the job saying "Yes, absolutely. I want to hear about shooting the machine-gun killer. You were actually four hundred yards away?"

Carl said, "The other one's a better story."

He watched Tony get up from the sofa and smooth out the front of his pants saying, "Can you hold it a minute? I want to check on Louly, see how she's doing."

Carl watched him go to the bedroom door and

put his ear close as he knocked and said, "Louly? Are you gonna be long? I have to go to the bathroom." Carl watched him fidget at the door, heard him say "What?" a couple of times, having trouble hearing her.

"You're paying for it," Carl said. "Go on in."

"I can hear the water running," Tony said, walking toward the door to the hall now, telling Carl, "I'll be right back," and left the suite.

The door closed and Carl pulled himself out of the chair, crossed to the bedroom and walked in saying, "Louly, where you hiding?"

She was in the bathroom. He saw her, the door open, stepping out of the tub full of foamy bubbles, the redhead naked and looking right at him as she reached for a bath towel, in a hurry to get it, but then more relaxed holding it in front of her.

Carl had the feeling she was deciding in these moments how to act with him, like a good little girl, mortified that he'd seen her naked. Or as Tony described her as being self-conscious, bashful. Oh, was that right? But not too bashful to shoot Joe Young that time at the tourist court, the day after Carl first laid eyes on her. He watched her turn around to dry her back.

Louly saying, "Are you still watching me?"

"I can't help it."

She dropped the towel, giving him a clear shot of her pert little fanny, and reached to take her green bathrobe from a hook on the wall. She kept her back to him slipping into the robe, showing some modesty, since he'd already seen that patch of red fuzz against her pure white skin. It looked like Louly was going to be herself with him.

She came out of the bathroom saying, "Where's Tony?"

"He had to pee."

"I never met a writer who was so polite and considerate." She sat at the vanity and began brushing out her hair. "And I never had a bubble bath, so I bought some, see what it's like. It's okay, has a nice smell, but all you do is sit in it."

"You miss a lot," Carl said, "living on a cotton farm." He stepped closer to see her in the vanity mirror, head lowered, her fierce strokes brushing her hair pulling her robe open.

She stopped brushing and looked up at him.

"I'm getting tired of these interviews. I've had to make up stories so they stay interested. I told one guy, a reporter, well, I did happen to run into Charley Floyd by accident one time, when he was living in Fort Smith. The guy interviewing me says, 'By accident, huh. Sure.' I said, 'If you don't believe me why should I talk to you?' he says,

'What were you doing over in Arkansas if it wasn't to see him?' Then I had to think of something right then."

"That you don't want him to believe either," Carl said.

"Yeah, and it gets confusing. I heard in Sallisaw Charley **was** there, in Fort Smith with Ruby and their little boy, Dempsey, and I did think of driving over to see Ruby. But they moved again and nobody knows where." Louly brushed out a few more strokes, stopped and looked up at him again. "You know what I decided to do? Go to Kansas City. They say it's some town, all kinds of jazzy places to see, and now I can afford to do it."

"There's a lot to see in Tulsa," Carl said.

She caught him looking into her robe and pulled the front of it together saying, "You know I have that five hundred they gave me for shooting Joe Young. I want to spend it in Kansas City, not some oil town."

"You want to see Tulsa and save your money," Carl said, "you could stay at my place."

She held the brush above her head.

"Stay with you?"

Carl watched the robe come partway open, but this time, looking at him in the mirror, she didn't touch it.

"I've got a two-bedroom apartment with a new kitchen, a comfortable living room and a big

Atwater Kent up next to the couch. A maid comes in once a week, cleans and does the laundry. Stay, I'll show you around town."

"Don't you work?"

"I'm taking time off to relax."

She stroked her hair twice, stopped and said, "What would people say, I was to move in with you? Like my mother, she finds out?"

"Don't tell her."

"How about your neighbors?"

"They don't care."

Louly said, "I hardly even know you."

"I'm offering you a room," Carl said. "You don't want to see the town, the hot spots, go dancing, it's up to you. You can sit on the couch and listen to the radio."

Louly said, "You'd take me dancing?"

Tony pulled the key out of the lock, closed the door and turned to see Carl Webster coming out of the bedroom.

"She's getting dressed," Carl said.

Tony stood there. "You talked to her?"

"She's thinking of staying in Tulsa a few days."

"Well, she can't stay here."

Tony said it right away.

"She can tonight, can't she, if she wants?"

"We only have the suite till six."

"They gave you a rate," Carl said. "You didn't pay any fifteen dollars, did you, Tony? You lied to me."

He was sure the marshal was kidding. Though not absolutely sure. Tony walked to the couch saying, "If that's what I told you, yeah, that's the full rate. I had it on my mind, 'cause if we go past six we have to pay it."

Carl said, "Where's Louly gonna sleep, in her car?"

"We arranged with the hotel, they're giving her a deluxe room for two dollars."

"You bring the little girl to Tulsa and you make **her** pay?"

"I'm gonna take care of it," Tony said.

"You work for a cheap outfit," Carl said. "But don't worry about paying her way, I'm fixing her up. Sit down, I'll tell you about the one, 'Gunfight at Close Quarters.'"

He was doing it again, putting him on the spot, manipulating him. The same thing he did with Elodie, brought her up and then cut him off from finding anything about her. Or he liked to hear himself talk about himself.

"No," Tony said, "the one I'd like you to tell me is 'Marshal Shoots Machine-Gun Killer from Four Hundred Yards.'"

"That's what happened," Carl said. "That's the whole story right there."

"The only time you used a rifle."

"The only time I've had to."

"I know it started with a bank robbery in Sallisaw. But why there? What was the guy's name, Peyton Bragg? I'd like to hear the details."

"They're hard to remember."

It was quiet in the room before Tony said, "Why don't you want to tell me about it?"

"I'll tell you," Carl said. "See how much I can remember."

You know that ugly one-eyed bouncer wears smoked glasses? They call Boo?"

"He turned his head," Tony said, "he was a good-looking guy."

"But his ugly side's what you remember," Carl said. "His given name's Billy Bragg, the kid brother of Peyton Bragg, the machine-gun killer shot at some distance."

"Right," Tony said, "Peyton Bragg," and wrote it down.

"Peyton worked stills. He'd set his mash, run it through the cooker to drip into jars his brother Billy would deliver to customers. Then Peyton'd go out and rob a bank. The time the law finally got on him he robbed the Sallisaw State Bank. You know why he chose it?"

Tony said, "Sallisaw's close to the Cookson Hills?"

"See, you know why. But that's only one reason. The main one, Pretty Boy Floyd had robbed the same bank—in his hometown, you understand—and only got twenty-five hundred thirty-one dollars and seventy-three cents. Peyton said watch, he'd rob it the same way Choc had, with a machine gun, and ride out of Sallisaw with a teller on the running board and way more cash than twenty-five hundred and thirty-one dollars."

"Where'd you get this, what Peyton said?"

"From the kid he had driving for him."

"What was his name?"

"I don't recall, but the one that went in the bank with Peyton was Hickey Grooms, armed and dangerous, Arkansas banks had five hundred dollars on him. See, Peyton was sore 'cause Charley Floyd was getting credit for banks Peyton had robbed. In fact at that time, witnesses were putting Choc at almost every bank robbery in Oklahoma. So Peyton's intent was to show him up."

Tony said, "They say Pretty Boy was supposed to have robbed fifty-one banks in less than a year."

"You know that isn't true," Carl said. "Peyton

and his partner are in the bank, Peyton waving his machine gun to get everybody's cooperation. Now they're in the vault loading sacks with cash . . . while the kid driver's sitting in the car revving the engine, wants to make sure it won't quit on him. He keeps watching the bank and doesn't see the police car drive past."

"But they see him," Tony said, "acting suspicious."

"So you know what's gonna happen," Carl said. "By the time the kid driver notices people looking toward him as they hurry past the bank, and finally turns his head to see police on the street he starts blowing his horn."

"What kind of car?"

"An Oakland. Brand-new eight the kid swiped off a lot in Muskogee. Peyton comes running out of the bank, gets to the car, the police yelling at him to stop, put up his hands, and he rakes the Thompson at them, shooting up parked cars, storefronts . . . His partner comes out with the bank sacks as Peyton's firing and the police shoot down Hickey Grooms he's barely out of the bank. Peyton's in the car now looking at his partner lying dead on the sidewalk, about ten thousand dollars of cotton money in the sacks."

"You learned this after, how much they took?"

"That's right, but the kid driver said in his statement Peyton knew about how much they had and looked like he was gonna try to get the sacks. The police and others were shooting at the car now, so the kid said he punched the gas pedal, 'held her down' and they got out of there."

Tony said, "You mentioned Peyton fired the Thompson."

"He killed one of the officers and a couple of people standing there. Once they're out of town it was a chase through the hills, no paved roads up there, we're following tire tracks and dust most of the time. The Sequoyah sheriff set up a roadblock near Brushy. Peyton busted through and killed a deputy. By the time they got up toward Bunch, the Adair County sheriff with us now—"

"Wait," Tony said. "What were you doing in Sallisaw?"

"Inquiring after Charley Floyd. I went there to talk to his wife's relatives. A cousin named Louise had written to him in prison."

"You mean Louly?"

"I didn't know her then. She wasn't there anyway. Her stepdaddy, Mr. Hagenlocker, said she'd stolen his car. I drove back to Sallisaw, the bank'd been robbed."

"So you joined the chase."

"I believe I was telling you, we got up toward Bunch, there was the Oakland off the side of the road, its rear end sticking out of the growth, the kid driver waiting there, putting his hands up as we approached him. He said Peyton had him pull off the road to hide the car, but when he did it got hung up in the undergrowth, why the ass end was showing like that. The kid said a car happened to come out of a road almost across the way, where there was a filling station had gone out of business. Peyton ran out and stopped the car—the kid said a woman driving—and rode off in it."

Tony said, "What make of car?"

"A 1930 Essex two-door, green, one the Adair County sheriff said belonged to Venicia Munson, an old-maid schoolteacher from Bunch."

"So you went to see her."

Carl wanted to say he'd get to it, all right? But kept his peace, wanting to tell this part the way he remembered it.

How he spoke to the sheriff from Adair County about Venicia Munson, the sheriff, an old boy, reminding him of his dad, the chew in his jaw, direct when he spoke but in no hurry. He said, "I've known Venicia since she was a little girl, more'n thirty years, but have no idea what she thinks. They say she almost ran off with an oil patch roughneck one time when she was a kid, but her old man put a stop to it. I never heard of her seeing anybody else. She don't talk 'less you talk to her first. She don't fix her hair or doll up any." The sheriff said, "No, I take that back. I saw rouge on her face the other day at the post office she was mailing a letter. She wouldn't be too bad she fixed herself up. Except she's I mean skinny, hardly any sign of breasts on her to speak of."

"Who you think she writes to?"

"I been wondering about that."

"You think she knows Peyton?"

"She could."

"They both like to hide out."

"I know what you're saying. Your hunches any good?"

"Sometimes."

They found the house at the end of a mile of ruts in a straight dirt road, through land swept bare by wind and drought, the house old, left over, Venicia Munson the last of her family to live here.

The green Essex stood close to the house.

Carl told how she came out on the porch as their four cars crept into the yard: two from sheriff departments, Sequoyah and Adair, one sedan holding the Sallisaw posse with their shotguns and rifles, and Carl's Pontiac, the kid driver riding with him.

"Look at her," Carl said to the kid driver, "and tell me if she was in the Essex."

"I never saw her good."

"It's the same car, isn't it?"

"It sure looks like it."

"Tell me," Carl said, "if Peyton stopped that car or the car stopped for him?"

The kid said, "What's the difference?"

"Did he threaten her with the machine gun?"

"He wasn't holding it then."

"He left it in your car?"

"I think he forgot it."

"He have a gun in his hand?"

"I didn't see one."

"Do you recognize her?"

"I told you, I didn't see her good."

Carl, with the Adair County sheriff, got out and approached the woman on the porch, touching their hat brims. Carl gave his name, told her he was a deputy U.S. marshal, and said, "How're you today?"

Venicia didn't say, she stood waiting, hugging herself with skinny arms, red circles of rouge on her drawn cheeks.

"Tell me," Carl said, "if you stopped your car to pick up a man on the road, not more'n a couple hours ago?"

She shook her head.

The sheriff said, "Venicia, this is Peyton Bragg we're talking about. A witness saw you pick him up in your car."

She said, "Whoever thinks he saw me's mistaken."

The sheriff said, "There's only a couple Essexes in this county I know of and this is the green one."

Carl saw the way she looked right at the man in his worn-out wool suit and tie, the plug in his jaw. Now she shrugged her shoulders.

Carl said, "You mind if we go in your house and look around?"

She said, "Why? You think Peyton Bragg's in there?"

"You know Peyton?"

"What difference would it make?" Venicia said. "You aren't going in my house."

The sheriff said he was sorry but they had to. "Peyton killed three people, one of 'em a police officer, robbing the Sallisaw bank, and shot a Sequoyah deputy at a roadblock." He turned and motioned to the others to come on, they were going in.

Now Carl told the **True Detective** writer how they searched the house, the upstairs, the storm cellar, poked through wardrobes full of family clothing . . . It was Carl who looked in the stand by the front door, wondering why there were so many umbrellas in it, and found the Winchester .30-30 among the black folds of cloth. It had a scope sight mounted on it and was loaded. Carl held it up to Venicia Munson.

She said, "It's mine. All right?"

Carl put the rifle in his car and came back to see everybody outside now looking off at the land, all of it dead to treelines in the distance, the closest maybe a quarter mile away.

Carl said to the woman, "Miss Munson, if you see Peyton before we do, tell him to give himself up while he's still alive."

She didn't say anything, but it got him strange looks from the others. The posse from Sallisaw walked back to their car talking about what he'd said to her. The Sequoyah deputies took their time, turning to look at the woman and comment among themselves.

Carl said to the Adair sheriff, "She and Peyton know each other. Before he robbed the bank he made plans to hide out at Venicia's." The sheriff frowned at him, working the chew in his jaw, and Carl said, "Peyton didn't stop her car on the road. She was there to pick him up."

"This is your hunch?"

"I got it from the kid driver. Only nobody told him about it."

The sheriff looked out at the nearest treeline and tugged his hat brim down against the late sun.

Carl said, "He'll be back tonight."

All Bunch had was a filling station, a sawmill that cut rough lumber, a frame church and a general store with the post office one of the counters, mail slots behind it on the wall.

Carl told this to Tony in the Mayo Hotel suite.

"We sent the kid driver back to Sallisaw with the posse, five of 'em packed in the car. They had to promise to keep their hands off him since he was just a dumb kid. We had the two Sequoyah deputies, and two from Adair County the sheriff got hold of. He's the one I was talking to, Wesley Sellers, if you want to write his name in your notebook. He's coming over to Okmulgee sometime, talk to my dad about the Spanish war and we'll shoot at crows eating pecans. Wesley brought us to his house and his wife fixed us egg and onion sandwiches and opened a can of deviled ham for whoever wanted to spread some on bread, while we decided how to lay for Peyton. One good thing, we knew he'd left his machine gun in the car."

"But he'd be armed," Tony said.

"We didn't have any doubt of that. We decided I'd be the one to go in the house, the last resort if Peyton got past the others spread around outside."

"You'd talk to her?"

"If I could think of something to say."

"How did you feel, face-to-face with the woman, knowing you or the sheriff's people were gonna kill her sweetheart?"

"Did I sympathize with her?"

"Feel sorry for her—this old maid with a bank robber for a boyfriend."

"She wasn't anybody to me," Carl said. "Soon as it was dark I drove up to the house, as if I'm visiting. I see her car turned around, the Essex, its rear end toward the house, ready to shoot straight down the road. I thought if the key's in it I'd yank it out. But I hear Venicia's voice—she's on the porch in the dark—ask me what I want. I have to get her in the house, so the others can walk up the road and take their positions without her seeing them."

"She'd know you weren't alone," Tony said.

"Most likely," Carl said, "but you never know. I told her I wanted to talk to her. She asked if I'd brought her rifle back, said I had no right to take it—the Winchester with the scope. It was still in my car, but I didn't tell her that. I said why didn't we go in the house and sit down. She said all right, I suppose curious, wanting to hear what I had to say, and took me through the living room to the kitchen and turned on the light over the table."

"She knows you're not gonna ask what you do around there for fun. I bet she broke down," Tony said, "pleaded with you to spare his life, only the second boyfriend she'd had in her thirty-odd years."

"No, but she surprised me," Carl said.

She asked him if he wanted a drink.

Carl said no thanks, and watched her open a cupboard to bring out a fruit jar of moonshine and two glasses and put them on the table. She said, "In case you change your mind," and poured herself two inches of the whiskey that looked no more potent than creek water. She wore a wool housecoat, green, like her car, that came to the floor and looked too big for her, the sleeves too long. She wore rouge, circles of it on her cheeks, and lipstick tonight, bright red in the light hanging above them. Venicia sat down with her back to the sink and cupboards and Carl took the chair to her left, to be facing the back door. He didn't like sitting in the light.

"You're a schoolteacher, uh?"

"And I drink wildcat whiskey," Venicia said. "What do you make of that?"

"There's no taste to it—it must give you what you're looking for. Peyton brings it?"

"When he remembers."

"What do you do, you run out and he's not around?"

"Honey, you're in the Hills. I can go a mile in any direction and pick up what I need for social occasions. You understand, I only drink when I have company." She raised her glass to him and took a sip, a good one, then touched the sleeve of her housecoat to her mouth. "What I'm always running out of are cigarets."

Carl took out his pack of Lucky Strike, popped a couple of cigarets to stand up and held the pack to her. Venicia took a cigaret and lit it from a book of matches she brought out of her housecoat. It said BE MOUTH-HAPPY on the cover, SMOKE SPUDS. Carl slid the pack across the table to her, its green wrapper close to matching her robe.

"If you're trying to get me to talk about Peyton, keep it up. But I doubt I can tell you anything you don't know. I will say one thing. Peyton gets to the house and sees you through the window, he'll shoot you dead." She raised her face to blow smoke that swirled in the light.

Carl said, "What grade do you teach?"

"All of them."

Carl said, "Peyton's already killed four people today."

"Yeah? You think I don't know what he is?" Venicia got up and came back from the sink with a tin ashtray. "You'll get him or you won't. You do, I'll have to go up the road for my whiskey." She drew on the cigaret again and said, "How many people have you killed?"

It was in his mind that he hadn't killed any **people** and said, "They were wanted criminals, fugitives."

"Aren't they people?"

"You say 'people,' I think of innocent people, not mad-dog ex-convicts and murderers."

"How many of those have you killed?"

Carl hesitated. "Just three."

Only three by that time, he told Tony. Wally Tarwater, the one stealing his cows; Emmett Long, in the farmhouse near Checotah; and David Lee Swick coming out of the bank in Turley with a woman hostage, the one Carl had approached from across the street telling Swick to let the woman go and drop his gun, and when Swick fired,

Carl pulled and shot him through the head at fifteen feet, the reason the Tulsa paper called it "Gunfight at Close Quarters."

Venicia was saying, "You shoot Peyton you'll be even with him, won't you? He did shoot a man in Tahlequah one time, fighting over some whore, but only winged him. The man survived Peyton's wrath."

She sipped her drink and smoked her cigaret and asked Carl, "Are you nervous?"

He said, "I'm all right. Are you?"

She said, "To tell you the truth, I'm scared to death."

"It's what happens," Carl said, "you get mixed up with a man like Peyton."

"You're the one scares me," Venicia said, "not Peyton. You know why? 'Cause you'd rather shoot him than try to bring him in."

"It's up to Peyton," Carl said. "What'd I say to you a while ago? You see him, tell him to give himself up if he wants to stay alive."

"Where am I gonna see him before you do? I hope to God he doesn't come, 'cause you'll shoot him down like a dog."

Carl was shaking his head telling her, "Uh-unh, we shoot when there's no other way to stop the fugitive."

"That's your excuse," Venicia said, "why you became a marshal and get to carry a gun. You like to shoot people. I think you get a kick out of it."

He didn't tell Tony what Venicia said—it wasn't a detail of shooting the machine-gun killer.

Carl kept it to himself, because that whole time they were tracking Peyton Bragg, it was in his mind that when they caught up with him and there was a gunfight, he'd have a chance of making Peyton No. 4.

He did, he saw Peyton as a number.

But was that bad, wanting to put a desperado out of business? It was what marshals did and he was proud to be one—even though his old dad thought he was crazy trading high risk for low pay. The only thing he'd ever felt after was relief that it was over and he was still alive. That time in Turley he was shaking after. The woman hostage fainted she was so scared and he thought he had shot her.

First relief, then later on he'd feel proud of what he did, the way pilots in the war, Eddie Rickenbacker, had German crosses painted on the side of his Spad, under the cockpit, proud of his kills. Rickenbacker had twenty-six. That German, though, the Red Baron, was the ace of aces with over eighty kills. They went up and looked for enemy planes to shoot down. Marshals went out to take wanted felons dead or alive. What was the difference?

He had made balsa models of the war planes when he was a kid. The German Fokker with three wings he painted a bright red.

Carl said when they heard the gunfire Venicia was lighting a cigaret. He jumped up but remembered the match burning her fingers—if Tony wanted details—and saw her drop it on the table. He told how the shooting was coming from the front and by the time he got to the porch the Essex was driving away from the house, the key in the car or else Peyton had it. Carl said he ran to the Pontiac and reached in to get the Winchester, the deputies and Wesley Sellers around front now firing at the Essex running away from them. Carl said he saw the red taillights come up big in the scope sight, aimed a little bit above the left one, the deputies yelling at him to shoot, and fired, levered the rifle to fire again, but the Essex had veered off the road, crop furrows slowing the car down till it rolled to a stop.

"The round caught Peyton in the back of the head," Carl said.

Tony, writing in his notebook, said, "Number four for you, uh?"

Carl didn't respond to that. He said, "A deputy paced off the distance to where the car went off the road and said it was four hundred yards, give or take."

"Did you consider it a lucky shot?"

"I hit what I aimed at."

"But at that distance—"

"It was more like three hundred yards."

"You see Venicia Munson again?"

"When I went back for my car."

"Was she crying?"

"I couldn't tell."

"She say anything to you?"

"Asked could she have her rifle back."

"You give it to her?"

Carl shook his head. "It was evidence."

Tony went to the bedroom door to check on Louly again. She told him she'd be out in two minutes. Coming back to the sofa Tony looked at his watch.

"She's been in there almost two hours. What do you think she's doing?"

"Looking at herself in the mirror," Carl said. "It's what girls do."

"There's something I want to ask you," Tony said, "about the gunfight at the roadhouse." He sat down again and flipped back a few pages in his notebook. "Everything happened so fast."

"You want to know," Carl said, "who shot the Wycliff boy, me or that one-eyed bouncer. I'll tell you, I think by the time Boo got around to shooting him rigor had already set in."

Tony grinned. "I know, I saw you shoot him first, and I'll swear to it in court. What I'm not sure of, you told Nestor if you had to draw your gun—you know, you'd shoot to kill."

"What bothers you?" Carl said. "You think I had my gun in my hand?"

"That's what I want to know."

"Why's it matter to you?"

"I'm writing the story, I want to be able to describe what happened."

"If I had it in my hand—when did I pull it?"

"I'm not positive you were holding the gun."

"But if I was," Carl said, "if I already had my Colt out, would I have been lying to Nestor about pulling it?"

Tony was shaking his head. "It's got nothing to do with telling the truth or not. They bust in with the car, you know any second they're gonna start shooting."

"But was I lying to him?"

"No—as I said, it wasn't about lying or telling

the truth. I guess it's what you say in that kind of situation."

"You were up on the stairs, had a good view. Tell me what you saw happen."

"Nestor raised his guns and you shot him."

"What's wrong with leaving it at that? Just telling what you saw?"

Carl left a few minutes later saying he was going to stop by the Belmont estate, see if he could have a word with the dad, Oris. "But listen, you want to ask the little girl about Charley Floyd, go ahead. I'll be anxious to hear what she says."

12

If your boy robbed banks, broke the law selling alcohol and shot different ones with every intention of killing them, would you protect him? Hide him? Carl believed most parents would lean toward making excuses for their boy and try to help him, but wasn't sure about the Belmonts, especially Jack's mother.

Carl called Oris Belmont's office to make an appointment to see him, but was told he was in Houston, Texas, this week. Carl had already checked on Mr. Belmont's personal life and wondered if he might be at the Mayo Hotel with his girlfriend. Carl decided no, not all week, a man who'd been a wildcatter and now ran a number of businesses. Or he could be home for some reason.

That's where Carl went, to their mansion among all the mansions in Maple Ridge, that rich area south of downtown Tulsa. He parked his Pontiac on the street and went up to the door. The six giant columns holding up the portico, as big as they were, didn't impress Carl; there were twenty-two columns across the front of the federal courthouse he entered almost every day of his life. He was about to ring the bell, but then decided to have a look around first, in the open about it, here in pursuit of a fleeing felon—Eddie Rickenbacker looking for Fokkers to shoot down, though he'd rather have the score of the German ace, Manfred von Richthofen, who'd press the buttons to fire his machine guns and another Spad would go down smoking, or a Sopwith Camel, the German the same age as Carl when the Canadian got lucky and shot him down. Walking past the side of the house he thought about the model planes he'd made and painted and was allowed to hang from the ceiling of the living room because Virgil liked to look at them.

He came to the back of the property and saw the swimming pool covered for the winter. He turned to the house—there was Mrs. Belmont on the patio standing with her back to him at a window, washing it with a sponge, a dish towel over her shoulder. The husband worth twenty million dollars and the wife did the windows?

She turned and Carl saw he startled her. He used a quiet tone of voice stepping up on the patio, touching his hat brim and telling who he was and showing his star. She didn't say a word. He asked if Mr. Belmont was home and it got her to shake her head. He said, "I'd like to talk to you if it's all right and you have the time." He paused and said, "About your son," just as a colored woman in a white uniform with a heavy coat sweater over it came along a walk between the patio and the swimming pool—pushing Emma in a wheelchair, strapped in, the girl's head hanging in the collar of a fur coat. Carl knew about Emma, how she'd gone in the pool without her water wings and almost drowned, her brain shut off for fifteen minutes before she was revived. The colored woman called to Mrs. Belmont:

"You washing windows again? Where you want me to put her?"

"Right there," Doris Belmont said and turned to Carl. "I'll talk to you." She hesitated and said, "Let's go inside."

Doris took him through the house to the front hall and up a staircase that had to be six feet wide to a semicircular sitting room that appeared lived-in and Carl believed was her dayroom where she spent her time by herself with this heavy, upholstered furniture; a decanter of sherry sat on a silver tray with stem glasses, the tray on a round table in the middle of the room. The windows looked out the back to the swimming pool and the lone figure, this woman's daughter head-down in the fur coat in late-afternoon sunlight.

Carl tried the edge of a deep chair and then sat back as Doris Belmont sank into the middle of the davenport and wiggled her fanny into the cushion.

She said, "You think Jack's here, hiding out?"

"It depends how you feel about him?"

"You see that girl out there? She can't walk or speak 'cause he let her drown, watched her drown, and we went and brought her back."

"You saw him do it?"

"I **know** he did it—God have mercy."

Carl looked out at the girl, Emma, about twenty now, her face hidden in the fur coat. He turned back to Doris.

Waiting for him, Doris saying, "I'll tell you something," then paused and sounded like she'd changed her mind saying, "I'm tired. I am **so** tired. You know why? There isn't nothing to do. I have two maids and the woman who takes care of Emma. This is her time off now, having a smoke with her coffee. You happen to have any cigarets?"

Carl got out his Luckies. He went over to her and struck a match to light hers and then his own, Doris saying, "Pour us a glass of sherry while you're standing there. Else I'll get you whiskey if you rather."

Carl said no, sherry was fine, saying, "We have

some at Christmastime." If Virgil remembered to tell his Texas oil buddies to bring a couple of bottles. He said to Doris Belmont, "You were gonna tell me something, and then realized how tired you are. Though you look like you're in good health."

For a stick of a woman with pale, sunken cheeks.

"But you don't have anything to do," Carl said, "except wash windows?"

"I was cleaning off something a bird left."

"Instead of getting one of the maids? I guess you've worked all your life, haven't you? I imagine you were raised on a farm?"

"We moved in this house," Doris said, "I got turned upside down. I mean it. Nothing a-tall's the same as any place I have lived. I'd go back to Eaton, Indiana, tomorrow and all that ever amounted to was hard times."

"What's Mr. Belmont say about it?"

"About what? My not liking it here?"

"Or having Jack on your mind—what he did."

"What the boy's done all his life, whatever he wants. You know why he tried to kill Emma? 'Cause Oris named his first gushers for the child, Emma Number One and Emma Number Two, and never named a well for Jack." Doris took a sip of sherry and puffed on her cigaret. She said, "You know what I do mostly? Make sure that decanter always looks about half full. It's cooking sherry, but serves my need."

Carl said, "You must talk to Mr. Belmont."

"You mean about Jack? Whatever I say Oris agrees in a soft voice patting my hand, then thinks of something to tell me, like he says they're talking about changing the name of the bank. Oris has a guilty conscience, but I'm not sure if it's for sending Jack to prison or 'cause he's still seeing this old girlfriend of his. One time Oris showed hisself, he said, 'Jack's so bad you want to hit him, only now it's too late, and when I should've been hitting him I was looking for oil.'"

Carl, trying to think of something to keep her busy, said, "You cook?"

"We have one I'm finally getting use to, a colored man from New Iberia, Lou'siana. Oris brought him from down there he was looking at oil property. We have all these people, the maids, the cook, the one takes care of Emma, all living here in this house. My mother comes to visit . . ." Doris shook her head, tired.

"You say Mr. Belmont agrees with you," Carl said.

"On account of his guilty conscience. I say, 'If Jack should come home, you won't let him in, will you? Or let him talk to you?'"

"What's Mr. Belmont say?"

"Says a course not."